Games of the
Strong
Glenda Adams

Also by Glenda Adams

THE HOTTEST NIGHT OF THE CENTURY,
short stories
DANCING ON CORAL, novel

Games of
the Strong

Glenda Adams

CANE HILL PRESS

Acknowledgements

This book was written with the assistance of a Senior Fellowship from the Literature Board of the Australia Council.

The Sacred Journey is adapted from *Lampah-Lampahan R.M.A. Poerwa Lelana.*

This book was first published by Angus & Robertson Publishers, Australia, 1982. Copyright©Glenda Adams 1982.

Library of Congress Catalog Number 88-063899
Copyright©Glenda Adams 1989
All rights reserved
Printed in the United States of America
First edition
ISBN No. 0-943433-02-9

Cover art by Robin Tewes

Published by Cane Hill Press
225 Varick Street
New York, N.Y. 10014

 Produced at The Print Center., Inc., 225 Varick St., New York, NY 10014, a non-profit facility for literary and arts-related publications. (212) 206-8465

For Caitlin

PART I: MOUNTAIN

They are detaining resisters and putting anyone suspicious under house arrest in preparation for the Games of the Strong, known as GASTRO. The Games are intended to reinforce the power of the Complex over its territories and undermine support for the resisters, of which I am one. The most dangerous resisters are being jailed.

It is a good time for our group to leave the Complex for a while, because we are certain we are on the arrest list. We have decided to go to Paradise, as tourists, making a detour up the Mountain to Rekkned especially for me. Secretly, I think I may stay on the Mountain if I like it there and if I fit in. The others in my group just want to leave the Complex and come back after a discreet interval to continue the resistance.

We are to leave tomorrow after my blood test. I have waited weeks for this appointment and can't cancel it now. I get dizzy and sleep a lot. The family gives me all the chicken livers and gizzards, but I still sleep and ache, today worse than usual. The others in the group say they understand my predicament and will wait for me.

There are five of us in my group: Serena, Anny, Leo, Wils, and myself, plus the driver we shall take for the trip.

Serena is a rose-red kind of person, voluptuous and strong. (VOSTRO, Leo calls her when he is feeling affectionate.) Sometimes the richness and fullness of her face and body stifle me and make me want to look away. When she moves she jars everything around her. Her voice is loud and uneven, and she laughs too heartily. She is a determined and skilled resister, however, and is in charge of our group.

Beside Serena's overwhelming substance, Anny is delicate, translucent, and slight. She enters a room and leaves with hardly a noise. Often you do not notice she is there. Her timidity, or deference, can be provocative in that it seems to demand cruelty or rejection, but she is understanding and giving, and people find it easy to be with her. Every group needs someone like Anny for morale and human kindness.

Leo is Serena's lover, although he does not like her much, and I think he prefers Anny. Whenever he can he pays Anny compliments and tries to talk with her, or with me. Serena often has to remind him that he belongs to her. He is the brains of our group and thinks up good strategies for resisting.

We first met Leo in a little cafe called The Rose Door in the center of the Complex, when our group was forming. He stood at the door, looking for the right table. Anny smiled at him, recognizing him from the description, and Serena beckoned him to our table, as if she had known him for a long time. He pulled up a chair between Serena and Anny, placing it intuitively rather closer to kind Anny and apologizing for being late. Serena offered him the bowl of little green peppers that stood in the middle of the table.

"I think they are too hot for you," she teased, and Leo felt obliged to take one. He took a small bite from the narrow tail of the pepper. Serena watched him, smiling. He took another bite and another, until he had eaten half the little pepper, with the top half, the thicker half containing most of the seeds, remaining.

When he hesitated, Serena took a pepper for herself and placed it in her mouth whole. She made a show of chewing it and did not shed a single tear, which was remarkable and shows how strong she is. She didn't even reach for a glass of water.

Leo then placed the rest of his pepper in his mouth and instead of swallowing it quickly, getting the seeds down before they could inflame his mouth, he seemed compelled by Serena's example to chew slowly. When he finally swallowed it, the tears sprang into his eyes, but he lacked the courage to take out his handkerchief and wipe his eyes or to drink some water. He sat there inhaling deeply through his mouth.

Serena banged her open palm on the table and laughed. "These miserable little green peppers are short and skinny. I prefer the red ones that are long and sweet. What about you, Leo? Short and skinny or long and sweet?"

Anny sat embarrassed, looking at her hands on the table. I caught her eye and I raised my eyebrows and widened my eyes. She burst into a fit of silent giggles that lasted the rest of the meal and prevented her talking to Leo. When Leo stood up to go, Serena stood up with him, and they left The Rose Door together. Because of the giggles, I feel partly responsible for letting Leo go to Serena so easily. But it is his fault, too. He should not have eaten the pepper. After that first meeting, Serena and Leo became lovers, as if Serena had intended it before she even met him. Serena keeps on saying that she is the perfect woman for Leo and that he needs her very much. When we talk about everyday things after a meeting, and if Leo is not with us, Serena describes in great detail what she and he have discussed, the food they have cooked, and how they have made love. Hearing all that makes Anny uncomfortable, and it makes me restless and unhappy, considering my own situation. I never get a chance even to talk to Lak alone, let alone make love to him. His mother and father and sisters watch us all the time.

Today I realized that Wils, who is Leo's uncle and is older than all of us, is in love with Anny and that he is eager for us to go on our trip, more because he might get a chance to sleep with her than because he fears for his safety. Wils was a famous fighter during the revolution and has even been commemorated on a postage stamp. Now, like most of those old revolutionaries, he is a respected member of the Complex and a successful businessman, although some of his old revolutionary friends are back in jail because they would not adjust to the new ways. Perhaps because he believes in our cause and is dissatisfied with the way the Complex is running things or because he is lonely and does not like getting old, Wils decided to join the new resistance. He is an adviser to our group, and his friendship protects us and makes us all less suspect.

I am a resister because I think the Complex disposed of my mother and father. Ever since they died, when I was quite young, I have been billeted with a series of Complex families, and at the moment I am officially staying with Lak's family, all orthodox and well-respected Complexers. I imagine the Complex is still waiting to see if I turn out all right or if I am like my parents, before I am given permission to live on my own. I like to believe that my mother and father escaped and may be on the Mountain, although the Complex has declared them dead in a car accident, and there are two graves marked with their names in the Complex cemetery, where I leave flowers. You would think if they were alive they would try to make contact with me, but they could be afraid to come out of hiding. I have nothing much to remember them by—really only a scarf, which I love, that was my mother's. It is blue and green like the sea or blue and green like the mountains and sky.

My new family constantly tests my loyalty to the Complex. They know about my parents, but I don't think they suspect that I am actually a resister and a member of a resistance group. They test my loyalty by complaining about the Complex.

"You can't even get handkerchiefs, the way you could in the old days," says Mother.

"Handkerchiefs are not top priority," I reply. "We are happy and free."

"Food is twenty times the price," says Mother.

"We are more prosperous than before. We must work still harder," I reply.

Even though it is so trivial, this kind of grilling sometimes bothers me so much that I report it to Serena and the others. My group says I am doing the right thing and that I should be especially careful not to join in the criticisms or give any hint that I am sympathetic to the new resistance.

But my new family is good to me, and it is still astonishing to me that I have fallen in love with Lak, who is the eldest son. I was not looking for anyone, and I am used to being alone. In fact, I expect it. I have no illusions. And true love, that intense and remarkable and continuing rapport between two people, is a rare thing. I believe you find it once or perhaps twice in a lifetime. I did not expect it with Lak. He did not appeal to me, mostly because he seemed ill at ease with me. Also, I was not comfortable in that house at first. Lak spoke seriously, trying to welcome me without being too friendly. My first reaction was panic. How was I supposed to live with this family? There was a terrible little fan in the corner of the living room making a terrible din so that it was impossible to hear anyone on the other side of the room or in the hallway. Now, as I pass by the living room, I often see Father and one of his visitors talking, but because of the fan I cannot hear a word.

After a while, Lak began to smile a little, to respond to me. We found we liked talking to each other and he would stay on at the dinner table even after he had finished eating. He seemed to like listening to me, and we began to look at each other after a joke. Because of Lak, I have blossomed and perhaps he has blossomed, too, because of me. There is a special bond between us.

Because he is kind, his family takes advantage of him, and his sisters tease him a lot. They always ask him to do things—to take them shopping, to make a difficult phone call, to postpone an inconvenient visitor. And he is shy, which pleases me. We have grown together slowly. Now, I am always waiting for Lak to come into the room, and when I bicycle home I pedal fast to get there quickly, hoping to find he is home already, sitting on that marble bench at the front, pretending not to be expecting me. He brings me intense happiness, and also great pain at the futility of it all. This has been the case for a year now.

The family sees to it that I am never alone with Lak. When

the resisters (not my group — we are thinkers) set fire to the news tower to try to sabotage GASTRO, Lak and I listened to the radio reports and found ourselves alone for about ten minutes. After the broadcast he asked me about my real family and the Mountainers, because I had once mentioned the Mountain and distant cousins in Rekkned. He wanted to know all about the Mountain, its topography and climate, and about my connection with it. I told him about my father's father, who gave me a copy of *The Sacred Journey* when I was a child. I have wanted to climb the Mountain and look into its living volcano ever since I read the stories in that book, and I need to belong somewhere. The others in my group have no interest in the Mountain and I do not blame them, but the detour on this trip will add several valuable weeks to our absence. I was so glad to feel Lak's interest that I recited one of the stories to him, first in the Mountain language, and then in translation:

Nuhadak nakibak aras jnin nednit ehak jnagidid Rekkned agatak, Ieragt ildke mena hubeka imak erumum jnedat hawas jni itel Amalp, analak adsepep nateded ejjnajnab kotas as: desi nasukar supak nubinarijjnunabbak. Madsepep uaw ajatak imak nesadeperas jni deperak jni hawas ludas jni Amalp jni towusam usaljni.

Once a year on the holy day all the Rekknedese, men and women, young and old, honor the crater of the Mountain, taking with them food and clothing such as headcloth, jacket, sash, and so on. These goods are thrown right into the crater as an offering to the god who dwells there. And thus the people are renewed.

That is what the sacred book says, and I know when I throw something into the volcano, I will solve my problems.

"Neila, why don't you feel you belong with us?" Lak asked. Then he implied that the Complex was a mess and that GASTRO was a useless affair. It made me sad to think that he was testing my loyalty even then.

"The Complex has improved our lot, and GASTRO attests

the progress," I replied.

Then Father burst in without knocking. He found us sitting at the table, close but not even our fingertips touching, in front of the radio. Father would like to be rid of me, I think. He and Mother are frightened that I will lead their son astray.

The family questions me about my job with the Complex—I teach the Complex language to foreign businessmen and other visitors, and I write publicity releases. I am actually very good at my work—it is easy for me. The family asks me who I know and who I see at work. They seem to want to make sure that I am spending every minute under guidance and supervision.

I think I would tell Anny about Lak and me, but she is Serena's friend, and she might pass it on, especially since I am partly responsible for her not having Leo. The others in my group would laugh at me and warn me against the relationship, given Lak's orthodox family and its closeness to the Complex. They might even use Wils's influence to get me transferred to another family, and I would die if I were in the Complex and not near Lak. Serena has often suggested that Lak and his sisters are actually paid by the Complex to watch me. I find that hard to believe, but I suppose anything is possible.

But I like my new family very much. I call the four girls my sisters, and unfortunately I have to call Lak my brother sometimes. My feelings toward him are not those of a sister. When I told them that I wanted to go on a little trip to Paradise with some friends, the family said, "Of course, you need a change, you are so pale." But while they seem to be glad for my sake that I am going, they also seem to want me out of the way and they are suspicious. The presence of Wils among my friends seems to reassure them.

I am glad that I am going because I am fed up with everything. I am fed up with resisting, with being lonely, with loving someone I cannot have, although it will hurt to renounce Lak and stay alone on the Mountain.

This morning I spent one hour trying to telephone Serena for instructions and three-quarters of an hour waiting for a bus outside the museum, staring at one of the new GASTRO posters. It showed the chief resister, whom I have never actually seen, with a grotesquely large head and the body of a male dog; his followers were ugly little goblins or devils. Sturdy young Complex men and women speared the chief resister through the mouth and toppled his followers like dominoes.

The roads were flooded. Children swam in the huge potholes, and cab drivers used the muddy water to wash their cabs. And the news lights continued to flash around the tower, proclaiming the might of the Complex and GASTRO.

I had just said good-bye to my student, Odi. He wanted to learn the Complex language so that he could trade with the Complex from his own country. His language is not perceptibly better after his nine months with me, and thank heaven I will never see him again. We did not even exchange addresses. He flipped up his clip-on sunglasses so that they formed awnings over his regular glasses and enabled me to see his eyes; we shook hands, then he flipped his clip-ons down again and drove off in his navy-blue Volkswagen. I wonder if this will happen with everyone I know all through my life.

Then, because I had not been able to get through to Serena by telephone and she had to give me certain instructions for the trip tomorrow, she turned up at the house in the late afternoon, much to my consternation. I introduced her to the family as someone I worked with, and Lak sat with us for a while. Then, when Lak went to ask that syrup be brought in and served to the guest, Serena gave me a few inconsequential pieces of information, which made me wonder at her foolhardiness in coming. When Lak came back she looked at him over her glass of syrup, smiling, while she tossed questions to me, to one side, about the Mountain and its climate and what she should take on our little holiday trip. Lak ended up raising his glass and more or less toasting my charming friend and colleague before he excused himself.

Tonight the whole family has gone to a wedding. I like them to go out and leave me, with just the servants out the back. I watched the girls get dressed in their ceremonial clothes, and I acted as dresser, doing up buttons and hooks and fetching things. They complained all the time about the bother of having to dress formally, but in the Complex it is expected if you are invited to the wedding or birthday of a prominent official, and I don't believe they hate it all that much. I had a moment to smile at Lak, all dressed up, too, escorting his sisters.

While the girls were still arranging themselves in the car, Lak came back quickly into the house. It took me by surprise. He came right up to me and held my arms. Then he held me against him.

"I am going to miss you, Neila," he said. "Perhaps one day it will be different between us, when the struggle is over."

"I am going to miss you," I said, and I started to cry.

"These are strange times," he said. "Take good care of yourself, and watch those friends of yours. I don't think I like them." He held both my hands in his hands, and he kissed me. They were calling him from outside and he left.

I feel elated, enormously relieved. But I still have to go on this trip, because of GASTRO and the arrests, and I have to go because it is impossible for Lak, an orthodox Complexer, and me, an outsider and a resister, ever to come together.

I have just been out through the fields. I rarely go out without a chaperone or one of the girls (except for meetings, when the family lets me go because they believe that I am going back to my Complex job to work overtime). I walked ankle-deep in the mud and found it comforting. I want Lak so much. I followed the little raised paths and walked among the local Complex people out with their children in their new clothes for GASTRO. I felt underdressed in my jeans and rubber thongs.

At dinner, before the family left for the wedding, we were all somewhat humorless and terribly serious. We passed food to each other, saying "after you" and "do please finish this, it won't keep until tomorrow," as if we were all trying to eat as little as possible and save everything for some other day. We all acted as if we had to be persuaded to eat. Yet I was ravenous. It was our last meal together before my departure. Could it be that they all care for me and are sad that I am leaving? The noise outside was extraordinarily loud. The Complex has handed out free firecrackers for GASTRO. Our Nassah was out there, having prepared our dinner and finished his duties, while we sat indoors somberly protesting we had had sufficient to eat and discussing curtain fabric and current window fashion, a subject that interested no one.

I am glad to be leaving this stress and strain. I have spent several years learning the manners and language of the Mountaineers, and I have studied the sacred book. It is all extremely difficult for an outsider to comprehend, especially someone from the Complex, where refinements of language and manner have become questionable in the space of one generation and associated with the old ways, which came to an end with the revolution. They have also been associated with the resisters, since dissidents and revolutionaries have retreated for centuries to the slopes of the Mountain to recuperate in the cool air before continuing their struggle.

Because I have a certificate showing that my father's father was a Mountainer, I have been able to pursue my studies free of suspicion.

Alagd jnin jnagidid Rekkned hirip nednow jnagid jnedat agtnok iwadu jnagid agdnom jnedat jni nubinagilj jnagid usiljn, asjnom nedop jnegtar deperam jni agilj ikodnajn nesasejapnubit iwadu neg ad anakodnajn kodnas hilubas deperam jninet jnas hataj agilj, kodsegak etap jnegtaras nedop nednow jnas-

Whenever a visitor or a stranger comes to the house, it is customary among the Rekknedese for him not to enter the house until invited to do so, and so the caller must wait until he is permitted by the householder to go in. If he really wanted to go straight in, no one would get upset because it would jni irutalma, diwa kiwadas neg nedop nesadesaljna iwadu nedop sanamuk, nagtanak jnelet edana jnabed iwadu belemuk neg nednow jnagid jnas jnegtar nulub deheram jni agilj adlak jnegtar hajjner. appear neither friendly nor polite, although never yet has anyone been heard of or known who dared go straight into the house and sit down.

I think that my cousins at first will accept me as a close friend and then, after they get to know me, as a member of the family.

We are still in the Complex after a terrible attempt to leave this morning. At seven o'clock I was at the hospital, as instructed, for the blood test. There were six others waiting at the "Closed" notice of the laboratory. We all carried a roomy basket or something large, which we all knew contained our specimens, except for the colonial-looking gentleman, who turned out to be a minor democratic ally, who carried his in a bottle in his pocket, wrapped in an imported handkerchief. At seven-thirty an office assistant in a flame-red dress pottered around behind the glass, straightening piles of papers and setting chairs at right angles to the desks. There were fifteen of us by then. We pressed against the glass and when the assistant opened the windows, we thrust our specimens and pieces of paper through to her.

The writing out of receipts in quadruplicate and stamping them with two different stamps took half an hour for the first seven of us. Then we went round the corner to wait for the blood to be drawn: ten minutes per person. Then three visiting allies, as anemic looking as the rest of us, arrived. They were led by a Complex woman of military bearing, who saw that they entered at the top of the queue. The minor democratic ally got sarcastic, which had the effect of getting him done last and me, by default, next.

At ten-thirty our group set out for Paradise, via Rekkned and the Mountain, only to be hit by a military Jeep full of young, laughing soldiers with red berets, who did not stop. Our car was wrecked. Trip abandoned for today.

Now we must find another way to leave. If we hire a car, the chauffeur's license will need an extra endorsement from the police, and they may refuse it. In any case, we can't hire a car until Monday because the police endorsement section is closed for the weekend, and Monday might be too late for us to get away.

I am feeling dizzy and faint and seem to need fifteen hours of sleep a day, and even then I don't feel well.

Today we set out before the sun rose, having borrowed a black Impala with red upholstery and trimmings from a colonel who is a friend of Wils. The colonel said that all the arrest instructions would be handed out tomorrow, and he joked about our missing all the fun.

Driving to A. took sixteen hours instead of the usual twelve, because of the bad roads after the floods. The heavy rain has stopped and the water is receding, leaving the half-grown grain ruined, particularly between L. and N. The Fielders were all out in long rows, knee-deep in mud, plowing or planting new grain. In some fields the new green shoots are beginning to show.

We stopped for lunch in N. A little old man came in selling GASTRO lottery tickets. He wore billowy white pajamas over his clothes, and when he stood in the doorway the sunlight shone through them, outlining his shorts and extremely skinny legs. So I bought a lottery ticket from him. Why not? But then I felt uncomfortable because he looked at me for a long time and thanked me repeatedly.

Serena wanted to go to the lavatory, which was at the back, and she had to pass through the kitchen. The cooks and helpers, chopping and pounding, pointed the way, crying, "Lavatory, lavatory." (Fielders still make a fuss over Complexers.) One young man, a kitchen helper, dashed ahead of her calling, "This way to the lavatory." He opened the door and shut it after her, as if she were getting into a car.

"Disgusting," she said afterwards, in such a loud voice that Leo had to tell her not to shout.

We are all relieved and even excited to be getting away from resisting for a while, except Serena, who insists on hating everything: the water is dirty, the people don't know the meaning of work, the animals are lazy, the people aren't cultured, the food might be all right for Fielders but not for her. I think of my father's father who always said: "Don't compare. See everything in its own terms." However, I must not forget that Serena is an accomplished resister.

We stopped like tourists in a rickety little roadside shop that sold delicate porcelain, spun silver, and handwoven cloth. These articles hung from the low wooden ceiling or were stacked closely on the shelves that lined the walls and formed narrow lanes running the length of the shop. As we edged our way sideways in and out of these lanes, the floorboards and shelves rocked slightly and pieces of the porcelain and silverware jostled against each other, making a tinkling sound.

Serena wanted to buy a series of brass bells displayed on a small round carved table in the doorway of the shop. Her voice and her breathing and her shifting about as she fought to have the price lowered caused some of the fine silver hanging near her to bump and chime.

Anny stood admiring a round porcelain pot. Leo came and stood beside her, his chin in his hand, as if he were memorizing the pot. He pointed out that it was slightly asymmetrical, and he thought he could guess the name of the village where it was made and possibly even the artisan who made it.

Anny was enchanted and looked up at him in her charming way. He then told her the meaning of the colors and the design. After that Anny wanted the pot, and with Leo's help she was able to have the shopkeeper lower the price enough for her to buy it. Leo picked up the pot to carry it to the car for her. But as he turned sideways to make his way around the little table with the brass bells, Serena turned suddenly, knocking the pot from

Leo's hands. It shattered on the wooden step in the doorway of the shop. Anny knelt on the floor and tried to retrieve the pieces in case it could be repaired, but when she saw that it was hopeless, she left everything lying there and quietly went back to the car. It is not like her to show her feelings like that or to leave any kind of mess, but Wils picked up the pieces and threw them away, apologizing to the shopkeeper for the disturbance. Serena told Leo he should have been more careful. Leo told Serena to shut up, and he said she was like a mad animal that destroyed everything in its path.

"I intend to destroy you," she shouted.

"You already have," Leo shouted back.

Their fight began to draw attention to our group, and Wils bundled us all back into the car.

Serena sat in front next to the driver. She told Leo she did not want him in the front with her since she could not stand him. It was a squeeze in the back, but Leo and Wils did not mind since it meant that they could both sit touching Anny. I had to sit squashed up between Leo and the window.

We talked and pointed at the countryside, excited at a particularly beautiful tier of green fields, a group of children playing by the road, or a cart laden with fresh fruit. It was useless trying to include Serena, who now refused to speak to anyone.

It is wonderful to be out of the Complex, but I am miserably lonely for Lak.

When it became too hot to talk or move, we merely nodded toward the field or the children or the cart. I fell asleep, and later they all teased me for sleeping the whole time with my mouth lolling open. I was embarrassed, and even angry at them. I hate being teased.

We are spending the night in a friend's bungalow. More smiling military youths with tin hats and rifles circled the house about nine o'clock. They are protecting us from resisters. The smiling silence that followed the "good evenings" was the sign to hand out cigarettes.

The rain is now pouring down. After dinner I ventured out alone, across the pitch-black fields, balancing on the little bridges that seem to be made of twigs, scrambling beside the rushing creek. I came across a group of people, Fielders, standing huddled in the middle of a muddy road watching a Complex film. They stood silently in front of and behind a tiny screen, about five by three, watching the reels shown in random order. I didn't stay. I seemed to make the people uncomfortable, and a woman alone is never a welcome guest.

We were driving along when the Impala came to a sudden stop in the middle of the road. Serena fell foward with a loud cry and shouted that the driver was a fool. She still wasn't talking to the rest of us.

A man stood before the car, a dead chicken in his upturned hands. He came to Serena's window.

"When you passed this way, some days ago, your car struck my chicken," he said. Rather than look at Serena he gazed at the ground.

"And?" said Serena. She opened the door of the car and got out. The man cast a quick glance at the rest of us, regretting that he had picked Serena to approach. He fixed his gaze once again on the ground at Serena's feet.

"You should pay the cost of the chicken," he said.

"What nonsense," said Serena. "This car did not come this way some days ago. And in any case your chicken shouldn't be on the road." She picked the chicken up by one leg. It hung stiffly, its neck bent in a sharp angle from its body. She placed it back in the man's hands. "It's been dead for weeks," she said.

"A chicken is expensive, and I must replace this one," the man persisted.

Serena stood for a moment. Then she struck the man on the side of the head. Anny clutched at Wils. He put his arm around her. Leo got out of the car and pushed Serena back in. He took several notes from his pocket and gave them to the man, apologizing. Inside the car, he yelled at Serena again for drawing attention to us so gracelessly. Serena is even more furious with him.

We passed through M., where several old friends of Wils are imprisoned, and we stopped to visit them. The guards clicked their heels as we went in through the gate. The chief warden had chairs brought into his office for each of us, and because of Wils he also had coffee brought in, while he noted our names and numbers. We discussed the present situation and the success and splendor of GASTRO, which opens this week.

My Mountainer certificate is most useful. I am returning to my family, we say, and since a young woman can't travel alone the others are taking me.

The cells of the jail form the four sides of a large square. Each cell gives directly onto the grassy open courtyard in the middle. The friends were sitting reading in the shade in the doorway of their cells. They welcomed us and gave us their chairs, and then sat on the grass at our feet.

One, a well-known writer, brought a flask of iced coffee from his room and poured us all a glass. He looked thin and quite ill. Another, who once headed a publishing house, brought out bocadavoes and cut them into slices. This man sat back and slapped his belly and told us that he had gained a lot of weight since he had been in jail. He said that life in jail provided all amenities except one. He laughed and looked at Serena and Anny and me in turn. Then he leaned forward and placed his hand on Serena's knee. Shortly after that he offered to show Serena his cell, and they went across the grass together to his room and did not reappear for twenty minutes. Poor Leo. But he really likes Anny. And Anny is beginning to get somewhat animated as the prospect of having Leo becomes clearer. Perhaps it was worth the broken pot. Poor Wils.

While we were waiting for Serena, the friends asked Wils about the current situation and teased him for being a proper Complexer now. They also enjoyed raising their eyebrows in Anny's direction and teased him about that.

"Not at it again, are you?" they said.

In the heat of the afternoon we parked the Impala and lay on the brown grass in the shadow of a high stone wall at the edge of the road. Everyone fell asleep quickly, but I am getting excited and less sleepy the closer we get to the Mountain.

I lay there repeating words to myself. There are nine ways to carry things: jnisjnagn, ditniju, napmejn, rujjnam, rusim, dibmejn, jnotnejjn, jnobopm, ijjnugn.

On top of the stone wall, near where we lay, stood a group of children. One of them maneuvered the string of a kite which floated high above us in the white sky. Another kite was also flying, some distance away, darting and dipping toward the first. The children flying this second kite were out of sight, presumably somewhere in the village on the other side of the fields. The children on the wall squinted at the sky, and the child holding the kite pulled it toward its rival. The kite string, which was impregnated with glass, cut into his finger as he tugged at it and played it out. He appeared oblivious of the blood beginning to run from his finger down his forearm. The string itself became red with the child's blood.

I watched the kites, repeating my words, until their strings finally came into contact. The strings rubbed together until one was cut and the kite attached to it fell to the ground.

We stopped at the house of a friend of Wils. Clearly a rich man. Also, I gathered, a resister, and very fat.

We drove up to his house and parked in the street. It looked like a modest place. A narrow block of land, a simple house made of the ordinary cheap bricks rendered pretty with cement painted pale pink. A door and two windows with shutters gave onto the street, and cement instead of grass formed the narrow strip between the house and the street. All very plain.

We rang the bell, which seemed to echo back through an enormous space. The door opened a crack and then, once the man had seen it was Wils and friends, he opened it a bit wider, just enough for us all to file in. Instead of finding ourselves in the simple little living room that the outside of the house promised, we were standing in a great chamber, a kind of closed-in courtyard, with a smoked glass ceiling that let in the light, a floor of wonderful square black-and-white tiles, and an extraordinary collection of plants growing from Chinese porcelain pots and hanging from the ceiling. There were marble benches and ornaments and statues scattered across the tiles.

The man led us, waddled I suppose is the word for the way he walked, to the other end of the chamber to elaborate wooden, double doors that reached from floor to ceiling. This, I realized, was the real front door. The other, that little rabbit hole we had crept in by, was a sham. Through the double doors we went into more rooms and hallways that stretched back and further back. Who knows how deep that narrow little block of his was? But inside we could have been anywhere. There was no outside or garden to this house. The walls encompassed it, like a fort, and inside was this warren of grand rooms, covered-in courtyards, fountains, everything. But all on one level. No staircases ascending. From the outside it must have looked like a hangar, a warehouse.

We sat ourselves down in one of the inner rooms. Food was brought. We feasted. And we talked about the resistance. Serena was still not talking, luckily. She sat eating, watching, listening, and looking disgusted at her companions and her surroundings. Leo, Wils, and the fat man talked and Anny and I, since we did not have anything startling to contribute in the way of high policy or thinking or a glorious past to offer, leaned forward and nodded to show we were involved and meant well. The fat man brought in two other men. The three of them and Wils had shared a lot during the revolution, but none had ended up in jail. Each had managed to make his way, doing very well in terms of money and status.

I was introduced as the daughter of my parents, whom the fat man said he had known.

"How did they die?" I asked.

"I heard it was an accident," he said. "I was out of the country at the time. Their hearts were in the right place. They could have done a lot. Beautiful woman, your mother, wasn't she, Wils?"

"They have left us their daughter," said Wils gallantly. "She is a good worker, with the same good heart in the right place."

It is always noticeable to me that no one calls me beautiful like my mother. They look for other attributes.

The fat man put his arm around my shoulder and had me sit next to him throughout the meal. When a new plate of food was brought in, and there were many of those, he searched for the choicest piece and fished it out and placed it on my plate. He did the same then for Wils on his other side, the way you have to if you are a host with excellent breeding. I felt like a little bird in the nest, and I did not mind that feeling, either. I did not mind him patting my head or touching my arm. It made me feel protected, like a child. I long for Lak, my hands in his and him looking at me in that way of his.

The fat man told us that the poet, Altner, had been arrested in the Complex, along with many resisters and other politically inconvenient people who may or may not be resisters.

I used to know Altner. We were students together, but we are not warm toward one another now, not because we actively dislike each other, but simply because we are different types, and I had ample opportunity to see him in action. At university he had already published a book of poems, and he had written a grant proposal which he submitted audaciously to one of the foreign embassies, requesting movie cameras and lighting equipment to make a feature film, for which he had also written the script and which he intended to cast and produce. The embassy gave it to him practically the next day. A truly amazing young man.

The fat man was not certain if Altner was actually a resister. Altner had been mainly absorbed in himself, his poetry and plays. He is one of those artists who can turn his hand to every-thing and does, and as a result, I think, has not reached his full potential in any area. I think it is a form of laziness of the brain, although he has great energy. He has written novels, poems, plays, and he has directed, acted, and studied religion and the martial arts for a while. He lives a bit like that, too, with many women. He leads a sensational life, and by sensational I mean that he has always tried for sensation, the experimenting with the senses. And he certainly does it with flair. He is a much-loved young man, loved by lots of women and students, but not by me. I find that I am suspicious of good-looking men who are also both talented and successful. And I have never liked men who have large followings of women. They seem not to have enough love in them to give to just one. Certainly part of the appeal of Lak is that I had to discover him. Altner walks along the street with a comet tail of women and admirers. He talks with his hands flying wildly and attractively, turning to the group on one side and then the group on the other side, wheel-ing around corners, the outer group running fast to keep up, the inner group marking time. The military could learn from this natural, free-flowing, instinctive drill formation.

And now Altner is in jail. He had been writing witty criti-cisms of the government and the Complex system, playful, not like Barm, the only writer I admire these days, who is a truly great writer burdened by his mission to criticize and reveal. I have always felt that Altner could change his beliefs easily, but I have to give him credit for going to jail. He had been warned to stop, and at one performance rowdies, presumably set up by the Complex, started throwing things at him. But he continued the performance until the fighting in the audience grew too dis-ruptive. His supporters started jumping on the rowdies and the theater was badly damaged.

"Which jail?" I asked, thinking I could perhaps help him. Regardless of my personal opinion, Altner did not deserve to be in jail.

"They couldn't use the regular jails for him," said the fat man, "not with his following."

We learned that Altner was in a house, a Complex house, one of those country cottage type of things. There was a staff of servants, and his family was allowed to send in good food and books. He could have visitors, too. He was also allowed out on weekends. And my sympathy diminished somewhat. I could imagine the lines of fans outside the house, the boys who hoped to be like him and the girls who were in love with him, and I imagined the pilgrimages that would be made to visit the martyr Altner. It made me smile.

"And do you know what he said?" the fat man went on. "As he was taken off from his home, from his sobbing wife and children and his mistress, who was visiting at the time, he said, 'Arrest? Wonderful. I need a break. Now I can get to the Proust and Joyce I haven't had time to read. Now I can complete my education.' "

Wils shook his head. "But his arrest should help the resistance nonetheless, shouldn't it?"

The fat man agreed. "We do need names."

After lunch we rested. The fat man, whose name was never mentioned, showed Serena, Anny, and me to a large bedroom with three double beds in it, the usual glorious tiles on the floor, and no windows. It was in the middle of the house, and I can't think how it got its ventilation. Since the room had no outside walls, it was cool and dark, and when I turned on a lamp we saw that the walls were totally covered by large paintings, larger than life, of naked women of all races, poses, shapes, and sizes, and all done in shining oils. They were not obscene, just luscious naked shapes lounging this way and that. It was breathtaking, overwhelming, to stand in that room and have these enormous naked bodies looming up to the ceiling. There must have been twenty-five canvases, thirty, in that room. Even with the lamp off, those bodies, the whiter ones, shone in the dark.

Serena was furious. "Disgusting," she kept muttering, which

was odd, considering her own performance with the pepper in the restaurant and all her innuendoes in the courtship and seduction of Leo. "Fat, oily, corrupt," she said, talking I suppose about our host.

"He is helping us all, remember," Anny said gently. "He obviously sells these and helps us with the money."

"And himself, too," said Serena.

"Perhaps his family has always been rich," said sweet Anny with the pure heart.

The road had been climbing gradually. The turns had been getting sharper. To get to the top of one ridge we had made thirty-four hairpin turns. In the late afternoon we were well into the foothills of the Mountain. It was no longer hot and steamy and we had to close the car windows. It was actually extremely cold. The road went up over one ridge and then suddenly down, down all those turns again, into a narrow valley, a little pocket, a crevice, a slit in the foothills. And suddenly all the heat returned, and we had to wind the windows down again. Dust seemed to hang in the air. Wils pulled at his collar (I still can't see why he wears his suit on a trip like this), and Serena made a big show of sighing and groaning and gasping at the heat. It was hot again, and the vegetation had also suddenly changed, from the dark greens of the foothills to the pale greens and browns of the bamboo which stretched along the top of the steep banks of a little river, deep and rapid and quite treacherous. Farther back were flowering shrubs, hibiscus, and even dusty lotuses in several muddy ditches. It was a microclimate, tucked in there, like an exquisite secret, a treasure. I loved the surprise of it, the miracle, that we could go from hot to cold to hot, and then back to cold again, so suddenly. And that little valley, with its rushing river, looked as if it intruded far into the hills, snaking around with its sunshine and warmth, perhaps right into the heart of the Mountain.

As we passed some cane fields Serena said she was thirsty

and ordered the driver to draw over to the shoulder of the road and stop. She took a long knife from under the front seat.

Leo groaned, "Here we go again," he said.

Serena stepped over the muddy ditch that divided the road from the field and she began to hack at the first row of cane. The pieces fell to the ground. She grasped the plant with her right hand and pulled it sideways. Then she raised the knife in her hand high above her head and brought it down angrily on the cane. With one tough plant she had to hack several times and she gashed her hand, between the forefinger and the thumb. She let out a cry and dropped the knife and sat down on the ground, pressing the cut to her mouth. She rocked back and forth and moaned as she sucked at her hand.

We all dashed from the car. Anny knelt beside Serena. She held her in her arms and begged her to say that she was all right. Serena moaned and sucked for several more minutes. While we waited for her to recover, Leo cut short lengths from one of the pieces of cane, and we each took a piece and sucked at it until we could continue our journey.

The Impala climbed back out of the miraculous valley and continued up toward Rekkned and the volcano. Some parts of the road, which winds interminably up and down and around those hills, seem to stay in perpetual shadow, so steep are the hills and so deep the fissures the road has to follow. Once or twice, where a little waterfall or stream had thrown water across the road, thin sheets of ice had formed and our driver had to slow down so that we would not skid. Yet down below, directly below us, in that little valley, were the giant bamboos and sunshine and heat. Once we stopped for the driver to adjust something, and I quickly got out and went to the edge of the road and looked down the hillside, to see if I could see the valley, but the trees grew up too densely and it was not possible to see far at all. It was hard to judge just how high we had climbed.

We came across a group of children crowding about in the middle of the road, and we were forced to stop. Three beautiful dragonflies with bright red bodies darted about above the children's heads. They wanted to fly away from the shrieking children. But each time a dragonfly started to fly off, it came to a sudden stop in mid-air and fell back toward the ground before trying once again. Then I saw each dragonfly was anchored by a thread, one end tied about its fine body, the other held by a child. The children were competing to see which insect flew highest, for as the insects flew up and away, the children jumped up and down and thrust their arms into the air to enable the creatures to fly a little higher. And in the clamor the dragonflies darted and jerked and reeled about, more and more frantically.

One of the insects seemed particularly determined to escape and kept flying toward a tree at the side of the road. It flew to the end of its tether, fell back, and tried again, throwing itself each time with all its strength against the thread which moored it. Finally, it strained so hard against the thread that it tore its own body in half. The two halves fell to the ground, and the child holding it, left with an empty thread, stamped in anger on the dead wings and tail.

The road ended at the highest village on the northern side of the Mountain. We were in Rekkned. When we arrived, just after dark, the houses were already closed up for the night, and there was no one sitting in the square or walking along the paths.

When we got out of the Impala we were hit by the cold. After the soft steaming valley, the air felt hard, almost solid. The cold set Anny's jaw shaking and she hunched her back and clasped her hands and breathed quickly. Serena stamped and moaned and held her cut hand against her, for the cold was making it ache. Her lips had turned bluish and her tanned skin was suddenly pale and mottled.

I was excited to be almost at the volcano itself and in the place that my father's father had left sixty years before. It felt good to be standing straight and I felt at ease with the soft gray of the earth beneath my feet and the cold night around me.

Serena looked about impatiently, then reached back inside

the car and sounded the horn. Anny begged Serena, in a whisper, not to make such a noise. She thought that perhaps the people of this village retired early and might be trying to sleep. Leo told Serena to shut up. Wils went off to find someone and came back with a man who told us there were beds in the travelers' refuge. He said we could stay as long as we wished, and when we wanted to climb the volcano, as all visitors did, he would supply the horses.

Rabas naratew usiljni imak akolakol, diwa dira arim nubmak happma-nubinahapma hajjnim nutem jni itel, enet nubinoruw imak jnagtnab-jnagtnab kotas jninet orep. Rabas jnalpak nedop iwawus neg at agejjnahas jnedat jni itel Rekkned ijlama jnisak rijjni jni nasjnekek niwud jnulegd jni nubijnalugt.

The horses from there are all very strong, because when they are small with the long hair of a foal, they already begin to climb up and down the mountain paths. Horses from overseas are not strong enough to be used on the Mountain because of the extreme steepness and deep ravines.

The refuge was a long wooden building with beds in cubicles running down both sides. In the center were a table and chairs. There was no fireplace. We were the only visitors staying there.

Serena investigated the length of the room and said, "What are we expected to do with no heat?" and she looked about the structure as if she might break off pieces of wood to start a fire.

"We must get some sleep," said Anny. She put her hand on Serena's arm, gently encouraging her to calm herself and rest after the day's journey and the accident.

We each chose our bed and then collected all the thin cotton coverlets from the other beds and piled them on our own. Everyone was watching who was where. Leo saw to it that he took the cubicle next to Anny. Wils was on the other side of Anny. Serena, seeing what was happening, took the cubicle on the other side of Leo. At the moment I do not feel like sleeping.

Tomorrow I shall search for my family.

Anny got into bed, quietly, without taking off any of her clothes and fell asleep immediately. Serena tossed and turned. She had been in bed for some minutes, muttering and shifting around and complaining about the cold. Then she announced that the cotton covers were useless and she might just as well sleep with a block of ice. She was still too angry to reclaim Leo, and Leo did not volunteer to warm her.

Serena got out of bed, threw one of the covers around her shoulders, and began to walk up and down the long room. The floorboards gave beneath her feet and creaked as she walked. She strode up and down for some time, like a warden, until Leo yelled at her to get into bed and stop making such a fuss.

Serena walked to the end of the room, just to show Leo that he couldn't tell her what to do; then she came up and sat beside me at the table. She was crying, with small gulps. Her mouth was wide open, the corners turned down. She looked ludicrous.

She leaned forward, resting her head on her right arm on the table. "He told me I was an animal. He said he wanted to drive me away, because animals only understand brute action. I want to kill him."

I patted her back to comfort her, and she turned to me, so that my arm was around her and she rested her head on my shoulder. Then, to my surprise, she asked me to watch over her until she fell asleep. She went back to bed and as she calmed down and was close to sleep, with me watching beside her, she said that she did not love Leo anymore anyway and would give him up soon. She said she had fallen in love with someone else.

I found some cousins this morning, and they have invited us all to stay. Since their house is not really big enough, the others have decided to remain in the refuge. But I am here. Their house is exactly the way *The Sacred Journey* promised:

Nubinagilj jnagid Rekkned asinub agatak imak jnagtnabjnagtgab, nubinelos jnuman rijjnudak nubinaejabjni sogtob jni deper jni agilj. Nubiduluak lejab nejnedawis nanasukas nepma, nakasjnub jni nepma uaw nanasukas nameridab nirases imak nejnegta-jnegtajni nubikiwadna. Nameridab asinub nanasukab lodod iwadu jnagiteb jneja kali nowab hirip nednil nubinudar nesadirahas jnijnan neg urat nesajnejanubit diwa jnisak nubibelka.

The houses of the Rekknedese are all very long. There is a narrow door situated in the corner leading into the house. In line with the walls to the right and left are placed benches. At the end of these benches are placed two beds opposite each other. In between these beds is situated the big fireplace. In the day the flame is kept low but at night it is increased because of the cold.

I try to speak in my most careful Rekknedese and I watch my manners, to show them all that I belong. I love them all. I ask the cousins about my mother and father. Pab, who is a second cousin to my grandfather, tells me he never met my parents, although word had reached Rekkned that they had died in a car accident in the Complex. They are surprised I do not believe the story. Upi, Pab's wife, remembers my grandfather and remembers him leaving Rekkned. And she remembers hearing that my father married a beautiful girl who was not from the Mountain. "And that always leads to trouble," she said. I did not know if she meant the beauty or the foreignness.

They don't seem to want to tell me much about the family, which hurts me. Perhaps it takes time for them to know me and feel at ease. But they don't seem all that interested. They press me for details about life in the Complex, which seems so exciting to them. They ask me who I know, what circles I mix in, and if I am going to marry someone important. I have so longed to tell someone about Lak that I actually confided in the girl cousins, who are about my age. I told them I was in love, but with someone impossible for me to marry, and I was trying to forget him. I told them he was an orthodox Complexer. "But you are a Complexer, too," they said.

I also said that I would like to stay in Rekkned, and they were puzzled. "What on earth for?" they asked.

The cousins are planning a big dinner for me and the others. They are pleased that Wils is important, and they are proud to show us that even here in Rekkned they have bought new clothes to celebrate GASTRO, now taking place so far away.

It is dusk. In the Complex at dusk Father turns out the lights and opens all the doors and windows. He says that mosquitoes are attracted by the light. When it is really dark, he closes everything up again and then turns the lights back on. It is hard to tell if there are fewer mosquitoes as a result, but it is certainly much hotter with the doors and windows shut. This habit of Father's annoys Mother and the sisters and Lak, who want the lights on so that they can see. But they never say anything to his face. When Father goes to the dining room to eat, we all open everything up. Father pretends not to notice when he comes back in. It is actually a very loving transaction.

There are five kinds of headache: jnegub, urejn, dosegd-dosegd, demum, rejnep.

When Pab or Upi speaks, I lean forward in an interested way and nod my head, hoping they won't tell a joke. If it's Pab, there is usually a joke, and everyone laughs, including eight-year-old Ileh, and I do not understand the joke if it is told too quickly. If I pretend to understand and laugh, the cousins turn on me and demand that I explain it. If I don't laugh, they point out that I haven't understood. It ruins the illusion of belonging that I am trying to create.

This morning I made a terrible mistake. I walked in front of Upi. She was sitting on the back step talking to a friend. I walked right in front of them and pushed past. I was with

Cousin Dum, who is my age and knows how to behave. She walked around to the side of the house and used the other door. Why didn't I think of doing that?

And last night I sat on the arm of the chair for a moment, while Pab was in the room. Young Ileh, who has already said that my shoes are wrong because you can see my toes through the straps, kindly informed me in front of everyone that I was doing the wrong thing. "If you hurt someone with your bad manners, it will find its way back to you and you will be hurt in turn," he said. I felt like giving him a smack.

When Upi says, "I am going to the next village," and pauses and then adds, "would you like to come?" I don't know what to say. I don't know whether she is only asking me because she is refined and polite and doesn't really want me to come, or whether she thinks I don't want to come and hesitates because she is refined and polite and doesn't want to put me in the awkward position of refusing. I have no idea what to do. Stay or go with her. I don't know how not to hurt her with my bad manners.

Just for a moment I remember a walk to the ocean with Lak and the sisters, when we all talked and forgot to test each other.

Today I am feeling miserable and lonely, and it isn't even breakfast time. I suppose it's because I have been trying so hard and don't seem to be getting anywhere. I got up at five o'clock and have brought my books to the table, and I've been working and writing for two hours. It was dark at first and I could hear the carts and animals and voices of the villagers passing by on their way to the market.

I am never certain when I wake up whether my Rekknedese will be brilliant or stupid or barely functioning.

There are fifteen words for smell: jetap, sujneb, jnigdes, ujnar, sajnek, sijned, ijnaw, betek, nijdap, seba, jnikeb, dignak, sarjemek, kima, jnekap. Some of them are coming from the kitchen at this moment.

Every day I go to the village sermon, delivered in formal Rekknedese. Not many people attend the sermon anymore. The priest has a crew cut, which makes him look different from most Rekknedese, coarser. Yet every day I get a fresh shock at the quiet refinement of his voice and manner. He is, in fact, the most refined person I have met so far. This is what he said yesterday morning:

"Outer refinement and good manners are difficult but not impossible to acquire. A Mountainer must be refined and have good manners and be polite all the way through, inside and out. Be refined. Be good mannered. Do not hurt anyone's feelings. Be perfect."

Every day the same chicken wanders in, jumps up on a chair, and falls asleep. The same "Crush the Resisters" song plays on the radio in the house next door. Clothes are washed. Someone has a shower. People stand and chat outside. The refined sermon on good manners and good feeling continues.

I lean foward in an interested way and hope the priest will not tell a joke. He has been kind to me. He listens to me read passages from *The Sacred Journey* and says I do well. I tell him I want to stay in Rekkned. He says, "Those who try to immerse themselves in an alien culture are misfits in their own."

"But I am not alien," I say. "Remember my father's father. And I have learned *The Sacred Journey*."

He smiles. "Nothing is the same. Everything changes. Even in Rekkned."

"I'll find a way to stay. You'll have to take me in," I said yesterday.

"But you won't be happy here. Go back to what you have discarded."

"Rekkned is what I discarded. I am coming back to Rekkned."

"No," he said. "Your father's father discarded Rekkned. Not you."

I am distraught. Where can I go? The day after tomorrow

we climb the volcano. I must take something to throw in.

This morning, the girls at the school were practicing their dances for a performance on Saturday in honor of GASTRO. The refined hero was a little girl in a pink cotton dress with a yellow tie around her waist. The clowns and the giants were also little girls. The hero danced in a most dignified way and thwarted the violent giants. Then she collapsed into giggles. The very young children came streaming from their classroom to watch the rehearsal and sat around the pavilion enthralled.

I search graveyards, and I ask about my parents. "They're dead," everyone tells me.

Jni nubinanis hirip nednow jnagid Rekkned jnasjni hagteb, asjnom nubinagiljaseregt nagir itel Amalp, nubinablanus nesadeperas, jni nubinhawas itel uaw enet jnas nubinagilj hiped nubinablanus nesasaldekas nowames.

In the past, if a Rekknedese died, then his house was struck with misfortune by the Mountain. The body was thrown into the crater of the Mountain so that those in the house might be far from the body they had thrown away.

There are six kinds of stomachache: kerum, dirirm, jenum-jenum, benek, jusjnum-jusjnum, jnupmes.

Why is it that I seem to be getting more and more awkward and shy? The cousins are sitting at the back talking to an old Mountainer who has just returned from the Field after an absence of five years. They are talking excitedly, catching up on gossip, and joking. The Rekknedese is too fast for me. And I'm too shy to leave my cubicle and go out past them to have my shower. I would have to go right through them, since they are blocking the passageway. If I try to join in, they will all have to speak slowly for my sake or change to the Complex language, in order not to hurt my feelings. Yet that would spoil it for them, which would hurt their feelings, and that would then hurt my feelings, which already have been hurt a great deal.

It is five o'clock. Soon, when the girl cousins come in, they'll say, "You haven't showered yet?" and I'll feel worse than ever.

The girl cousins teased me last night about Leo, in front of everyone. They think he is the one I am in love with. Why did they need to hurt me like that and go against everything in the sacred book? It was not considerate, kind, good-mannered, or refined. I suppose I must get on their nerves. I must seem clumsy and dense and slow. Perhaps I should go back to the others in the refuge.

Last night was the party for us visiting Complexers. Wonderful music, but no dancing. All the guests sat for hours and hours in chairs set in rows. Like a waiting room at a railway station. (There are eleven ways to sit: logtnork, arik, jnesjnegt, jnolsjnodem, jnilsjnidem, jnisjnegtn, jnajegt, hubmid, sototn, jnilsjnadem, jnasjnalpm.)

I was asked to sing "Crush the Resisters." I couldn't bring myself to do that, even to allay suspicion, so I sang the Complex Song instead, all four verses, which pleased them. Then they asked me to make a speech about life in the Complex. I gave a subtle resister speech, hoping to reach them, to let them know that all was not lost, that I belonged, that Mountainers did not have to bow to the Complex. I spoke in my best Rekknedese:

"Harnaisimet agnadapeh ikurovel. Usnaaikunames nas-naplosus. Nat jnalasek nin suawigt nat usajan ilitnek." I would sacrifice my very life. I expect it of myself.

I was wearing a dark pink cotton blouse and white skirt. When I had finished my speech, the sides of the blouse, right to the waist, were wet with sweat. Sweating is not good-mannered.

When I had finished, Pab called out, "Now tell us how life is in the Complex. The movies, the clothes, the food, the parties." He turned to Wils. "And tell them in the Complex that even here we are celebrating GASTRO."

Wils made a speech about progress in the Complex, and he

and the others sang "Crush the Resisters." How could they sing those words and make those gestures? They need not have done it. I suppose they know best how to show loyalty and not arouse suspicion.

In bed after the party, the cousins told me that Anny was as refined as a Mountainer, a Mountain princess. I am jealous of the praise.

"It's because Anny never speaks or does anything at all," I said.

They shrugged to let me know that it was more than that. Then, so that my feelings would not be hurt, they said, "But you are more refined than Serena."

But it is not enough. I must try harder. And my feelings are hurt.

I bicycled with the girl cousins to a nearby village. "Why do you bicycle as if you're in a race?" they asked. I remember bicycling home to Lak.

In my absence, the others have worked out their problems, or so it seems. Serena has retrieved Leo. Anny didn't put up a fight, and my guess is that Anny has accepted Wils. The four of them are sitting at the other end of the table as I write. Their conversation is becoming more and more tiresome. Serena is bringing the subject around to sex, as usual. Wils moves even closer to Anny, who responds sweetly. I feel like a chaperone, here in the refuge. I am only staying here tonight because we will climb the volcano tomorrow and we need to get an early start. The man has just come to tell us he will bring the horses at four o'clock.

"Four o'clock," said Serena rudely. "Whose idea was it to come here?" Everyone knows it was mine. "We should have gone straight to Paradise and had some fun."

I pretend not to hear and keep on writing. The volcano is my last hope. I will throw in my mother's scarf.

It was still dark when they brought our horses. And it was freezing. Colder than any other night. "This is crazy," Serena kept muttering. Perhaps the others agreed. I think they were all wishing they had gone straight to Paradise.

We rode up through the village, following the narrow path that wound up to the crater. Serena's horse was restless and uneasy. It skipped and started and kicked little rocks loose. Wils, so dapper with his feet on the ground, looked miserable on a horse. He sat like a sack. Anny, Leo, and I rode ahead, with Serena and Wils clattering up a little way behind us. Serena made no effort to control her horse or move with it to help its ascent. She had looked at no one and had said nothing, apart from muttering, since getting up.

The trees became sparser and more stunted as we climbed. We reached a small level patch among the boulders and gravel and stopped to wait for Serena and Wils. Anny was disturbed by Serena's apartness, as she always is. She has to have everyone happy or else her pale face puckers into a strained little frown. Her distress at Serena outweighed any excitement she might feel at being next to Leo and at climbing the famous volcano.

Serena stopped her horse just below us. "I'm not coming," she called. "You go on without me. I'm going back to the refuge to sleep. This whole tour was a stupid idea."

Anny was upset. "You must come with us. It's only a little bit farther. Then we'll all go to Paradise and then back home and everything will be the way it was."

Serena ignored her. "I'm going back," she said to Leo.

Leo shrugged. Wils, gallantly or otherwise, said he would go back with her. Leo beckoned to Anny and me, and we continued up the path. We climbed to the outer rim of the old crater. Looking back we could just make out the shapes of Serena and Wils below, as they picked their way back to the village. Ahead, stretching before us, was the gray dusty sea of the old crater, and in the middle rose the new brown cone containing the life of the volcano. The red of the fire inside the cone glowed against the dark sky.

We rode down into the sandy sea, slipping and slithering on the wall of the outer crater. On reaching the flat ground, our horses broke into a gallop and raced toward the cone, kicking up clouds of dust. At the foot of the cone we dismounted, for it was too steep for the horses.

Anny turned to Leo nervously. She looks awful when she is distressed. She looks nonexistent. "I can't let Serena go back like that," she said. "I have to go back to see if she's all right." She held Leo's arm. "Please don't be cross with me for leaving you. I see why you shouldn't go back, because you really want to climb the volcano. You two will be all right together."

She pulled at Leo's arm to get his approval. I could see she irritated him. She irritated me.

"Why should I care what you do?" Leo shouted. Anny cringed. Leo was shouting at her as if she were Serena.

"Don't be angry," she said timidly. Then she left.

It seemed so silly. Anny likes Leo, but was going back to Serena, who I can't believe she likes all that much. I love Lak, but there I was with Leo, sharing a profound moment of my life, climbing the cone of the volcano, into which at least some of my ancestors had thrown their offerings and their dead.

I was suddenly terrified. I scrambled on all fours among the rocks pulling myself up toward the golden glow that, as I drew nearer, seemed to cover the whole sky. At the top I was almost too frightened to look. I lay on my stomach and edged forward and looked down into the black pit. It was cut and patterned by the liquid rock, boiling and moving and jumping and spitting. I looked into the bright red depths and felt the warmth on my eyes.

I could see shapes within the red rock. I threw in the scarf. It disappeared in a puff of flame before it even touched the lava. I followed the movements in the rock trying to make out what they had to tell me. As the sun rose, the shapes grew fainter and I had to strain to follow them. It made me dizzy. I sat up and slid a little way down the inside of the cone to get closer to the red. I didn't want to lose the shapes. And I didn't want to go back. The red of the lava was turning gray in the daylight, the shapes were disappearing, and I could no longer follow the movements in the rock. I slid closer.

"Easy there," said Leo, and caught me by the belt.

"Let me go," I yelled and struggled to slide away from him.

Leo didn't let go. He hauled me out of the cone, and he held me. He put both his arms around me and held me against him. And I cried and cried. I have never cried like that. I didn't want to stop, but of course after a while I did.

The sun had risen. The shapes had gone. They had told me nothing. I had learned nothing. I was exhausted from the experience.

Leo and I sat at the edge of the volcano. He kept his arm around me and I liked sitting close against him. We talked a bit about my parents. I said I still wanted to find out the truth about them. Leo said that the car crash really was an accident. He said my parents weren't all that important as resisters. They only wrote and talked. If they had traveled around giving shows and making speeches and actually subverting the Complex, they would have been arrested and sent away somewhere. I would have been sent with them. As it was, the worst that could have happened to them if they had lived would have been jail for a while or house arrest or some other harmless means of teaching them a lesson. That's what Leo told me. He said if I did not believe him I should ask Wils.

It is hard for me to give it all up. I am terribly disappointed to learn that they weren't even important resisters. I don't know whether to believe him. Why all the fuss about me, then? The surveillance, and the billeting with an orthodox family?

Leo is a good man. What I can't fathom about him is his strength and calm and kindness (apart from his bursts of temper, which don't frighten me—I rather like them) and his inability to give up Serena, who makes him miserable.

For some reason, I am not as depressed as I would have expected.

I asked Wils about my parents.

"They weren't important, dangerous I mean, as resisters. It was an accident," he said. He did not want to talk about them and that made me uneasy.

This morning we left Rekkned and the Mountain. I have decided to go back to the Complex. I will give up resisting. I will leave my group. I will tell Lak I love him. I will become a real Complexer.

Perhaps that is what I learned from the volcano. I am still exhausted from it all.

Overnight at A.

To R. Ferry to Paradise. Carsick. Overnight in Paradise. Very pleasant. I can see why everyone likes it so much.

Toured around. We happened to meet a troupe of young singers from the Complex on one of the many goodwill tours organized for GASTRO. The singers were making stops at certain points and performing. They sang beautifully. They had completed a visit to a cigarette factory and were taking out their instruments for some singing and dancing in the back courtyard to demonstrate brotherhood. Out of good manners we all joined in. We got into a circle and clapped and sang. The old men who worked in the factory, dressed in their best shirts for the occasion, were reluctant to hold hands with their employers and with us strangers and dance in a circle.

The singers sang "Crush the Resisters," the Complex Song, and "Long Live Paradise and Its People." They were traveling in a bus driven by a man who had spent six years fighting with the revolutionaries against the old order. Now he loved the Complex and he loved driving the bus. After the singing and the dancing, he backed the bus into our Impala and scratched and dented all one side. (By now, we all knew to hold Serena back.) Since we had just affirmed friendship in song and dance, we accepted the damage gracefully.

I no longer care who does what to whom. However, the accident means we all have to slide into the car from the right-hand side, since the doors on the left no longer open. But we are getting used to it.

Ferry back to R. Overnight at P.

We arrived back in the Complex. The others dropped me off at my family's house. I didn't bother to ask about the next meeting, since I intended to give up the group, and they didn't mention it either. Serena actually gave me a hug and said, "Good luck."

I hoped Lak would be there. Of course, the family couldn't know just when I'd be arriving. The fruit trees by the gate were heavy with ripe fruit and I wondered why it hadn't been picked.

I found the front gate locked. I peered through. No sign of anyone. I went through the side gate. A Complex official, as if he were expecting me, came out of the house. I greeted him in the right way, but hastily, because I wanted to get past him, into the house to find Lak.

"There's no one here," he said.

"What do you mean? They must be here. They're my family." I could hardly breathe.

"They're resisters. The whole lot of them. We took them away. You have helped the Complex."

He said they had a new place for me to live and a new job at a higher rank. I sat down on that marble bench outside the front door, breathing in little groans. The official said I need no longer pretend to be a member of a group.

Pretend? I am crushed. I had no idea.

I am dizzy all the time. I would willingly sacrifice my life. I expect it of myself. But Lak will need me. He will be trying to find me. I have to find out where they have sent him. Now I must join a resistance group.

My blood test is normal. I did not win any prize in the lottery. I go to my new job. Official translator and news writer. They keep saying they are pleased with my group's goodwill tour to Rekkned and the Mountain, and I have been given a certificate of merit. I have no idea where Serena and the others are. I do not know if they are real resisters or spies.

My first assignment is to edit the official account of "The Games of the Strong" in the Mountain language for a commemorative volume. I look through it. I do not even try to amend the language, to improve and polish, to have it make sense. I do not try to make it truthful:

GASTRO IN RETROSPECT

In the midst of frantic mess outside and great pressing inside a sun shower fell, a metal bird hummed o'erhead in purplish sky and then a brass band hitting the sides of the arena opened the beginning of the Games of the Strong in the wondrous Complex.

These are the palmy days of the Complex and the Complexers knew the whatabouts. They were well meaning that the opening ceremony was crushed and stressed, the places not being easy obtainable.

The Complexers were not unlikely to thinking a way. Apprehending the inside's opening was not of easy access because of sparse tickets, the outside's happenings were there to behold.

The faces of all were happy, with no resisters longer in our midsts. The good people crammed to the gates to enter, then rejected, walked (because cars and buses were far parked) to grass with picnic foods. What a thing. With their perspiring sweats, and hungry mouths. So much goings on. What a thing.

Young ladies, gorgeous in their straw heads and best GAS-

TRO frocks waited for young men multifaceted in their dark glasses with ticket plus spare ticket. And many love matches at first sight were made that day, remembering that GASTRO also means love.

Inside much pushings for not enough seats, trying to glimpse even a little the goings on. A rare and gorgeous sight: the flags, the colors, the new plastic grass so green not dead brown.

On that very grass the loyal contingents trod: Complexers, others, and the democratic allies major and minor, swathed in robes of GASTRO colors. Public applause for them all. But the star was the GASTRO queen in a baroque dress plus alluring gestures and kisses thrown to all seers.

PART II: PENINSULA

I have been writing the news for the hourly news summaries in the Department of Information, and I do them quite well. Serena works with me, her desk facing mine. Wils is now the Information Minister and he is my ultimate boss.

The summaries are not difficult to write, but because of the constant deadlines, I am exhausted at the end of the day. The news comes in on the teletype machines and it keeps on coming, rolls of paper curling out covered in words. If I go away from the machine beside my desk for longer than five minutes, the paper and those words keep spilling out, and can completely cover the chair. Sometimes, when I am engrossed in typing my summary, the paper coming out of the machine covers my feet, and when I get up I trip over it and tear it and then have to spend precious minutes sorting it out and taping it all back together.

I have begun to have a dream in which the hourly deadline is approaching. It is usually six o'clock. At five minutes before six I find I have not prepared a single line. The paper from the machine has rolled out all over my chair and my desk and the floor. I crawl around the floor searching for the end of the roll so that I can start cutting up the news items, reading them, and composing the summary. I begin to read this mountain of news, only to find that the words are in a language I do not understand. Often this dream wakes me, and once, recently, I woke and found myself already sitting up, trying to get out of bed to get to work.

I think my father once told me that dreams like this are a way of proving to ourselves that we are survivors, that we can indeed live through terrible times. I usually feel that such dreams merely reflect sheer terror.

I also dream that my legs get hurt, that a leg is crushed by a stone and I am lame. I limp. This is probably because the old steel desks in the office are falling apart, and many of them have pointed or rough edges. I am always snagging my clothes and bumping and bruising my thighs and knees and shins, and often I go to bed with my legs aching.

There has been an uprising of resisters on the Peninsula and the machine is full of it. I have to give at least half my summary to the developments. We are trying out a new style of writing, to see if it engages the people. Before, we wrote in the official style: "An uprising was reported and immediately thwarted today. No mercy shall be shown to the resisters, although the strength and kindness of the Complex continues to be manifested," and so on. Now, we are to try a lighter tone: "There's good news today from the Peninsula. Our brave boys have trounced a cowardly and ill-organized group of resisters and brought back twenty-one dead and three maimed."

Of course, it is awful to have to write either way, but of the two I prefer the old way. Once you have learned to do it, you do not need to think about it much and it is so doctrinaire that no one can be moved or inspired by it. The new way requires a degree of enthusiasm, at least until it has become second nature. If the people respond well to the new way, then I suppose we shall keep on turning out the "our boys" stories.

Serena and I type away at our summaries. Neither of us mentions our trip to the Mountain and what happened afterwards. Nor do we mention Wils or the others with whom we traveled. All this time I have desperately wanted to know about Lak, but I still have not found anyone I can begin to ask, and I am always searching for a plan. I still do not know if Wils is really a resister, as I believed all the time that he and Serena and Anny and Leo and I were together, or if he is a loyal Complexer who was pretending to be a resister. Serena, I now know, is a Complex spy. Her job on the Mountain trip was to watch Leo and get him. And she succeeded, because he seems to have disappeared. Anny, too. That means Wils must be a Complexer, or he surely would have saved Leo, his own nephew. I still do not know if our Mountain trip was to avoid arrest and save our lives, or to spread genuine goodwill for the Complex, or to get me out of the way while they carried off Lak and his family. I still do not know.

I now live in a small hostel or dormitory for young women with Complex jobs. It is good luck that I have the room at the end of the terrace upstairs. It is large and quiet, and I only have to join the others in the dining room at meals and when there is a group meeting. There are ten of us here. The bad thing is that Serena is in the room next to me. Ostensibly because the weather is warm and sultry, but I think really because it has been ordered by Serena's secret police, we all keep our doors open. Each room has two doors. One leads onto the front terrace, overlooking the street, where we can sit and read or talk, and where our breakfast is brought every morning — coffee in a glass and bread with chocolate sprinkles or without chocolate sprinkles, according to the rate of inflation that week. The other door leads to the smaller back terrace and stairs and bathroom. After breakfast the office van comes and we all are transported to work.

If we close the doors of our rooms it means we have something to hide, so none of us closes the doors. This means that the rooms are like corridors or general rights-of-way for anyone who wants to get from the back terrace to the front terrace. The only way to the front is through someone's room. Since I am at the end, I get a minimum of traffic, except for Serena who traipses through my room like a chambermaid. She is chronically unable to be alone. I cannot protest, because indeed I do have a great deal to hide.

Sometimes, however, I experiment. I close the doors and time how long it takes for Serena to knock. Usually about two minutes. She needs me to set her hair, help pluck her eyebrows, measure a hem, give her change of a note, borrow a book, admire a blouse, or console her about the behavior of a new boyfriend. If I am resting, she will just sit on my bed and file her nails and look through my things to find something to read until I show signs of waking up. Sometimes she thumbs through my old copy of *The Sacred Journey*, pronouncing the words in a ludicrous way.

All this is torture for me. There is nowhere for me to go. There is a bathroom, but with ten women sharing it, I cannot stay there long. Whatever I do on the terrace is in public view. The stairwell at work is always too crowded. Anyway, it is used mainly for petty business and I have no material transactions I need to make.

I think my strength now is to sit still, and I am feeling stronger. I am able to wake up in the middle of the night to write and make my plans. I normally do this under my bed with the covers hanging down all around and a flashlight or small lamp under here with me. I do not want anyone to see a light coming from my room. I use the old trick of a pillow in my bed and blankets lumped up all around it, and it looks pretty realistic. I make no sound at all. Just as the oars of a boat on a calm night sound as loud as a shout, so the turning of pages sounds deafening in a silent house. Luckily I have done some news broadcasting at work and was taught to turn the pages of script silently. I got the idea of going under the bed from Barm, who is still my favorite writer, an admirable man, strong character, brave. He wrote his first two novels under his bunk while he was in prison, and his writing inspired a whole generation to rise up and throw out the old regime. He was young, the same age as I am now. That was during the revolution which succeeded fifteen years ago. But he is no longer an official hero, unlike Wils, because after the revolutionaries established the Complex and it was firm, Barm continued to criticize. He criticized the men who had been revolutionaries alongside him, who threw out the old regime and formed the Complex and Territories, COM-PATER. Surprisingly, Barm's work and biographical information about him are still available in some bookshops. The Complex should ban him, if only for the ideas and moral sustenance I am getting from him.

I have been reading the works of as many writers as possible, especially works of fiction and nonfiction that deal with the revolution. I still hope to come across the names of my parents. Barm's work stands out. There is nothing, of course, that deals with the present resistance, which the Complex claims to have ended, although today's writers who are clever enough, and there are not many, write about the past in such a way that it stands for the present. They put the present in historical dress. But they have to be careful. If they are too explicit they are sent to jail. I have always thought that my own mother and father wrote plays and tracts that were popular enough to be dangerous to the Complex and to have them imprisoned.

The playwrights write historical dramas and the performances are packed. Altner is one of these, or was. The newspapers have been forbidden to mention his name and his work. That is why I still do not believe the resistance has been wiped out. That, and the fact that the stairwell at work, for example, is always crowded. The architects should design stairwells with water fountains, sitting areas, private booths, the chairs screwed down to the floors, of course, and ashtrays, also screwed down.

A miracle has happened, and I have also been reprimanded for my careless work on the commemorative GASTRO volume. Actually, it was not an official reprimand. It was Wils, of all people, who came to my office to give me some friendly, fatherly advice, after all these months. It was the first time I had seen him since the Mountain tour, but beyond smiling and saying "Wils, how nice to see you," in a calm way, I gave no sign that we had traveled together all those weeks. It is not that I want to protect him. It is because I do not know anymore whether he is a resister or a spy. I hardly know what I am myself, what I am hiding from whom. And there was Wils descended from his lofty office, come to tell me to pull myself together. It is true that my work on the GASTRO volume was less than dedicated, but I also think that Wils wanted to see me, and that he wants something from me.

The miracle had already happened. I had received a letter. It was crudely written in Rekknedese. The mail opener assumed that it was from some relative of mine on the Mountain and therefore harmless. The Mountain and I and the goodwill tour are still mentioned around here. So he passed the letter on to me without entering it in his book and without reporting it or having it read first. I thought it was from one of the cousins, and I wondered what would make them get in touch with me unless they wanted something from the Complex, like a movie magazine or drip-dry fabric or something. And I began reading:

> Neila, my sweet one. How is your situation there? Good I am sure. All of us here in this house are healthy and do not lack anything. Neila, I am writing this letter while listening to the radio. Do you remember how we used to listen to the radio together? . . .

The letter was from Lak. I wanted to run to the stairwell with it and read it in peace, but Serena, who never seems to leave the office even to go to the bathroom, had stopped typing her article and was watching me, so I sat there and forced myself to continue reading it calmly in front of her.

> Recently mother and father and the sisters went up to their new village. They had to go on foot. The air was wonderful because they got the breeze from the sea, even though the little village is high up among the hills. In the village they feel calm, because of the fresh air and

also because the people there seem calm, different from where you are now. But they would rather be with you, I'm sure. As for me, my thoughts keep remembering you. How much more wonderful if you were by my side. I keep thinking of the times, in the past, when we were often together. I always felt joyful when you were near me. Now I am always counting the days until you will be with me again. . . .

"It is good news, I hope," said Serena. She had come around to my desk and was looking over my shoulder. "How are things on the Mountain?"

"Just fine," I answered, and went on reading, in front of her.

While Serena is fairly adroit with various international languages, she did not pick up the Mountain language at all while we were there. She is totally scornful of the territories and their cultures. They are my peculiarity. I was still puzzling out how Lak came to be writing in Rekknedese. Although the letter was stilted and quaint, the language was passable, and I wondered how he learned it.

"What's that word?" said Serena, pointing to the word for sea breeze, *duarnijna.*

"*Duarnijna, duarnijna, duarnijna,*" Serena repeated and laughed happily.

Sometimes I think I could kill her. "Serena, please," I said, imagining that she would now rush around the building singing that word and letting whoever keeps track of such things know that I, Neila, received a letter from the Mountain. I might just as well have stood up in the cafeteria at lunchtime and banged my spoon on my tray until I had everyone's attention and said, "You will all want to know that a letter was received by me this morning. It was written in the Mountain language by a Complexer I am in love with, who was recently arrested as a resister and imprisoned somewhere. It may be a love letter or in code and can be viewed in my office." Or I could just pin it to the notice board. Or turn myself in.

"*Duarnijna, duarnijna, duarnijna,*" Serena said again, this time to the messenger who had just come to collect the outgoing mail.

He grunted at her. "What's that you're saying?" he asked, a little too interestedly, I thought. I must watch out for him.

"It's Mountain talk," said Serena guffawing. She laughs like a seal barking. "*Duarnijna.* It means sea breeze."

Of all words. I believed I could work out where Lak was from that description of mountains and sea breezes. I wished I had lied to Serena, told her it meant something else, but I have resolved to tell as few lies as possible, partly so I can keep track of what I say. It is easier and safer to tell the truth, because then there is nothing to have to remember. And partly I try to tell the truth because I believe in telling the truth.

"Serena, please, you're embarrassing me, poking fun at my people and their language." I thought an ethnic appeal might work, since the ethnics are supposed to be equal now.

Is Serena doing all this on purpose, or is she stupid? I have been writing the news lights for several weeks now, and she is only asked to do it if I am called to a meeting. I have been wondering if she is jealous of me. It is hard for me to believe that she could be, since I have always regarded her as the clever one.

"*Duarnijna,*" she said to me.

"And *aket* means village, and *rigdes* means little, and *urarek* means always, and *gane* means wonderful," I said, thinking I would confuse her. Then I started reading the letter aloud, in a refined Mountain voice, singsong, and Serena collapsed into barks. That was when Wils walked in, accompanied by his assistant. The timing could not have been worse.

"Wils, how nice to see you," I said.

He nodded at me. Serena stopped her noise immediately and leaped to attention, looking ready to salute. Her office demeanor is more disciplined than her conduct outside, on the trip, for instance. Wils nodded at Serena and she relaxed and stood at ease.

Wils certainly exerts power these days. His assistant stayed by the door. I had never seen Wils behave in this official way. It was marvelous. I liked seeing Serena jumping through hoops. Wils raised his eyebrows at her.

"A letter was received by Neila," she answered. "From the Mountain. The Mountain language is amusing. Neila was teaching me some words, like sea breeze, but what was the Mountain word for that, Neila? I have forgotten."

The messenger was standing there in the corner, still. As I said, I might just as well have gone up to the cafeteria and banged the tray and made an announcement.

Wils nodded at Serena and she sat down and worked on her article. Wils turned to me. He acted in a friendly way, but gave no sign that the three of us had been on a special mission together, that we knew each other somewhat intimately.

"What news from the Mountain?" he asked me. I was still holding Lak's letter. Serena's typing meant that she could not hear him or me, but I still did not know what to answer. I did not know what his question was asking.

I looked straight at Wils. "The same as ever. My relatives, of course, praise the Complex indefatigably." That might seem like a lie, but it was not, because it was also true. The cousins are no doubt still praising the Complex, so it will not be hard for me to remember I have said that, because it is the truth. What was implied was that the relatives and the letter in my hand were connected. And that was less than the truth. I spoke without irony, and I searched Wils's face to see if he was giving me some kind of sign, some indication of where he stood and what he wanted from me. But I could not read his face.

Wils asked me if I would like to accompany him to lunch. I had to, of course. What I liked was irrelevant. Wils's requests are orders. I was still holding my letter. Serena was typing. The assistant was by the door. The messenger had disappeared. Wils smiled at me and took the letter. What could I do? Grab it back from him, revealing that it was not what it seemed? He looked at it as we walked together along the corridor, the assistant following. Wils smiled again. "A fascinating language, isn't it?" he said. What are your relatives wanting that we have here in the Complex?"

He laughed and I laughed along with him. "I haven't finished the letter yet, so I don't know if it is an eyelash curler or a magazine with pictures of movie stars or a post-natal girdle," I said, and we both laughed some more as we walked along, like two diplomats sharing a little private political laugh. "Could I have the letter back?" I asked.

Wils hesitated a moment then gave it to me. "You can let me know what they want and we can have it sent up to them," he said. Then he turned to his assistant. "Remind Neila to tell us what needs to be sent to the Mountain."

I think Wils had been intending to pocket the letter. I think he is a loyal Complexer after all, an enemy. But he could not very well say, "No, you cannot have your letter back," without showing me that he did not trust me. And I could see that he needed me today, since he had come so conspicuously to get me himself. That is why we were walking along the green carpet to the lounge, not the cafeteria, but the lounge, which is where you go when you want to be seen and when you need the people watching to learn something. Otherwise it is the stairwell, where transactions are made, usually trading. Someone needing a bedroom suite for a daughter getting married will trade some prescriptions for hard-to-get medicines, for example.

But Wils could never duck into a stairwell with me or anyone else. He always had to carry out his transactions in public. But he still could have chosen the cafeteria rather than the lounge, and I wondered what was going to happen to me.

First, the reprimand.

"You could go far, do a lot for us," Wils told me quietly. He did not lean forward in a conspiratorial way, but he spoke very softly and I found I was half lip-reading. "But you will want to pull yourself together. You are liked here and it is particularly pleasing when a woman shows that she can take the responsibility of a man. It sets a good example. You are wanted to represent us at the conference.''

One thing we all learn is to avoid the active and personal when we speak. And no orders are actually given, as in Wils's fine statements, ''You will want to pull yourself together,'' and ''You are wanted to represent us at the conference.'' Will I want to, indeed, and am I wanted, indeed. I get memos like that all the time from superiors and other departments: "It was thought that you would want to see this draft text and rewrite it . . ."

Lak's letter was then safe in my pocket. I know I can help him. Even without Wils's reproach, I would have pulled myself together. Because of the letter.

Wils told me that he was also going on a tour of the territories, after the conference, first to the Peninsula. He said he thought I would want to accompany the official party and write the speeches. He said he had been impressed by my composure and speech-making on the Mountain trip.

People in the lounge were looking at us. At Wils, actually, because he now causes a stir wherever he goes. And I suppose they were looking at me, too, wondering who I was. Several people who wanted Wils to notice them came up to us and bowed, and went on. Others wondered when they might have a word with him. Wils waved them away. They all looked closely at me, perhaps to see if I were someone who could help them get access to Wils and his favors. I have very mixed feelings about the tour. I want to find Lak and help him and the family, and all this official business will hold me up. It is possible that Wils is elevating me to the public eye deliberately, so that I am powerless and am kept busy writing those awful speeches. It is also remotely possible that he wants me to help the resisters by writing speeches with double meanings, like the speech I gave on the Mountain. But I doubt that possibility. And it is possible that he believes that I am a loyal Complexer and would want the honor of helping the Complex as much as possible. Or, he could be protecting me from something by displaying me publicly with him, to let it be known that I am not to be harmed. And I must say that all day today, despite my suspicion of Wils and everyone else, I felt protected by Wils's invisible presence. The word has got around quickly and people are nodding to me and bowing slightly.

I have not been able to finish Lak's letter until now. I am in my room and Serena has finally left me alone.

Neila, if we were together tonight as we used to be at the old house, I would ask you to come with me to see a festival. It is a pity you missed it last year, and this year you must try not to. And another pity is that Anny and Leo are here. I found them a few nights ago on the road. The bicycle they were riding broke in the middle of the road and they both fell. Imagine, Neila, Anny falling all over the place and Leo on top of her. But luckily it was not serious, just a little scratch on the leg or the arm here and there. Anny and Leo had not found a place of their own so they had to go round and round staying one night here and one night there, and I had been trying to catch up with them. I wanted them to spend the night with me. Anny is now exceedingly thin, because her thoughts are in such turmoil. Perhaps they need the mountains and a sea breeze, too. My thoughts are in turmoil, but they do not make me thin, rather the reverse. I eat because there is nothing else to do. Corn mainly. Let me know when you are coming, Neila. I am missing you and longing to see you. When you come, bring a little present for me, Neila. Enough, I am sleepy. My greetings to everyone in your house. And my embrace for you alone, Lak.

How does he know the language, even roughly like that? He has certainly written a letter that makes him sound like some

Mountain relative of mine. I feel like rushing to the Mountain immediately to find him, but now I am suddenly thinking that even though he writes in Rekknedese it does not necessarily mean he is there. I must get out the atlas and look at the territories, to see where there are mountains that could get a sea breeze. And corn. What does the letter mean? What festival?

I hear Serena calling out "Lolico" to some of the others downstairs. LOLICO is Long Live the Complex. The whole population is currently being trained to shout this out at gatherings, at school assemblies, and in the home as a prayer before meals. Variations are developing. LOLICOWORKER, for instance, is Long Live the Complex Workers. LOLICOID, I say. Long Live the Complex Idiots.

Serena has been out at a reception, and I am under the bed. I hope she goes straight to her room and does not put her nosy self in here. She has taken up Lolico as she takes up all the latest fads, as if they will die out without her help. She says Lolico in the morning, at night, and as an all-purpose exclamation during the day, as in "Oh, Lolico, I dropped the eraser into my typewriter." She probably says Lolico to her men in bed.

That could have been the last thing I ever wrote. Serena has been in my room. She came along the back terrace, tiptoeing, not clomping normally, which told me she was up to no good. She certainly is not the type to be worried about waking me up. "Lolico, Neila," she whispered softly at the door. I had turned off my flashlight, and when I heard her coming I just lay there. The terrace light was on and threw some light into my room, but fortunately it left my bed in the corner in deep shadow. It also meant that Serena, coming from the light into my dark room could not see clearly. She came in, stood still, then walked to my table, I think. I had left the atlas on the table, but luckily not open. Then she lifted something up, possibly the atlas, and put it down again. What does she want? I was afraid that she would see that my bed did not have me in it and that she would find me stupidly lying on my side on the floor under my own bed. I can think of no explanation of why I might be here. But she tiptoes out again. And I can hear her now humming and singing in the bathroom. As I said, she is certainly not the type to worry about interrupting other people's sleep. Imagine the lights, written by Serena: "OFFICIAL COMPLEX SPEECHWRITER FOUND WRITING SUBJECTIVE LITERATURE UNDER HER BED ... LITERATURE HAS BEEN BURNED ... BED HAS BEEN FUMIGATED ... SUBJECT JAILED."

If ever I am in danger of being discovered, my plan is to take all my writing to the bathtub and soak it. The ink will run and I will throw off my sandals and trample the pages to a mush. Then I will form them into a ball, a large ball, which I will explain is a sculpture. (We are encouraged to be active in the plastic arts and to exhibit our works. In fact, any piece of art made is required to be displayed.) I will put it out on the terrace in the sun to dry in full view of the populace and Serena. "Why did you need to write on it first?" they will ask, when they detect that the smudges of blue were once words. "It is part of the deeper meaning," I will reply. "Words that are no longer words. Words that have merged into a harmonious whole. One word." And when it is dry I shall paint it the Complex colors and coat it with varnish, and I shall put it on a long stick. And I shall call the piece, "Lolicop." Suck a lolicop today. I shall dedicate it to the Complex police and have it installed in the lobby of the new police building. And perhaps I shall be awarded a police medal for commemorating their force with artistic originality and energy. I like to think of all this writing on display in some form.

Or perhaps I shall go quietly to jail.

I have been told I am to do the news lights from now on. What excellent luck for me. The whole Complex will see my writing on the news tower and maybe there is a way I can send messages to Lak or the resisters. Perhaps Wils is behind the promotion. Writ-

ing the lights is prestigious work, and yet it is easy. All I have to
do is write seven headlines every hour, condensing the hourly
news summary even further. Now Serena will struggle with the
summaries and I shall just write the lights. They go like this:

LOLICO ... PENINSULA UPRISING QUELLED
... 21 DEAD, 3 MAIMED ... CAPTORS TRI-
UMPHANT ... RESISTERS IMPRISONED ...
MAJOR DEMOCRATIC ALLY PRAISES COM-
PLEX AND PROGRESS ... ECONOMY SOUND
... COST OF LIVING DOWN ... LOLICO.

The tower around which my headlines will go was the gift of
a major democratic ally for the Games of the Strong. In stairwell talk, the tower has come to be called the Major Democratic
Erection.

Today I went past the old house. I was on my way to an official
meeting with Serena, who still goes everywhere with me. I pass
by the house as often as I can without attracting attention. Each
time I expect to see Lak and the family there, with nothing
changed, as if nothing had happened. I expect to see myself go
in and sit on the bench and wait for Lak. At least the sight of the
house confirms part of my past. Yes, there is a house standing
there. If they had really wanted to send me crazy, they could
have had a false front built on the house, or knocked it down altogether, so that my memory would seem like a mad person's.
Yes, the house where I spent several years, happy enough, is
there. And yes, my family has definitely disappeared.

There are new people there now. They seemed to move in immediately, and they must be important in the Complex because
of the car with the chauffeur sleeping in it that is always parked
in the driveway. The bench is still there at the front, and the
ceramic pots with their succulents. And the fruit trees bear
fruit. But it is all somehow messier. The place looks unswept.

The driveway has cracks across it that have not been patched. If it is not patched, then it is going to get worse with the first big rainstorm. Lak's family was meticulous about that kind of repair. They took care of their things.

"I hate this street," Serena said as we went by. "You can practically smell the resisters." Then she laughed. "The smell lingers after the rotten fruit has fallen from the tree and has been thrown out. For a while, anyway."

I thought that some of the children playing on the street recognized me. They did not wave, thank goodness. Although Serena knows it was the house where I was billeted, I do not need her to suspect that I really am a resister and to be reminded that I still have ties to this street and this house and this beloved family.

I ignored the children, although I used to talk to them a lot. And actually I am surprised they did not wave. They liked me well and could not have forgotten. Of course, they get their ethics hour at school where they learn about the treachery and downfall of the resisters. Nevertheless, the removal of Lak's family and its replacement by the new people must have caused a stir on the street. Now that I think back on it, it seems to me that one of the boys picked up a stone and pretended to throw it at Serena. Or was it at me?

The Complex is corrupt in all ways. Posters have been up for weeks, advertising concerts by visiting international stars and artists in honor of GASTRO. One poster announced that David Oistrakh would play Beethoven's violin concerto. I was able to get a good ticket through my office. Father used to put that concerto on repeat on the family's old record player every night and sit in the dark listening and smoking his cigarettes. "I am trying to get to the bottom of Beethoven," he told me once. I went to the concert to remember him and to think about this life of mine. After we were sitting in the packed hall, and it was well past the time for the performance to begin, an official came out and told us that because of illness Mr. Oistrakh was unfortunately unable to visit the Complex. We were to hear substitute artists. The fifteen-year-old daughter of the Minister of Transport sang some lieder and her cousin, also fifteen, struggled through the whole concerto. To my amazement, whether out of fear or good manners, no one complained or showed anger. No one got up and left. We all sat there, through the whole thing, applauded at the end, and then went home. We are all corrupt.

I was sitting with the well-known observer of Complex affairs from abroad and the famous literary and social critic from the Complex. It is part of my job. We were sitting on the front porch of the critic's house, with glasses of tea on the little table at our knees. I had slipped off my sandals under the table and was resting my bare feet on the cool black and white tiles of the porch floor. The flowers in the garden were all blooming in the sun, and all sensible people were indoors taking a midday nap. But we were sitting up discussing the current situation, or rather they were. The observer from abroad had only limited time. I was trying to keep my mind on what they were saying, but it was boring and tedious. True, I might have learned something. But the general assessment of the overall situation and the on-the-one-hand-this and on-the-other-hand-that got so tedious that I could have screamed. If they had stooped to gossip I would have listened. Not only is gossip easy to listen to—a certain minister's wife is having an affair with a certain ambassador, or this education official who has an incurable illness and has gone abroad for treatment has left her husband alone and he has set up house with the ward of his first wife—but it is also the way I learn most things.

I was sitting there lumpishly looking at my feet and suddenly thought I was going to fall off my chair. The chair itself seemed about to throw me off. I thought it was the return of my old illness in a more virulent form. I was extremely alarmed and was trying to put together a sentence like, ''Will you please excuse me? I need to go in and lie down,'' when I saw a little crack open up and run right across the tiles under my foot and on under the critic's chair. It was an earthquake. The three of us stood up and went out into the garden. The critic was saying, "The situation in the Complex, then, is ambiguous," and the observer from abroad was saying, "Ambiguous in several senses," and without any break in the talk we stood in the garden in the hot sun for a minute or two until the earthquake stopped, then we went back to our chairs on the porch. The cracks across the tiles were fine ones, and I had heard nothing crashing down inside, no cups falling off shelves, which is one measure of the severity of an earthquake.

There were fifteen of us eligible for promotion, twelve men and three women. One of us would be chosen. We all knew it would be a step up, but we were not certain just what the new job would be. They took us into the seminar room where the first round of interviews was to take place. There was a rectangular table in the middle with fifteen chairs around it, one chair at one end, two chairs at the other, and six along either side. It seemed to me to be a significant arrangement. We were told to go in and sit down anywhere, and yet I knew they were watching to see who went where. One man, whose name I learned later was Smithy, went straight for the single chair at one end of the table, and that action defined his end as the top. The rest of us discreetly scrambled to seat ourselves as near to the top as possible. I ended up two seats away from Smithy, on his right, and felt I had found an appropriate spot, not too aggressive, not too withdrawn. The two other women shared the bottom of the table. It made me feel both glad that I was not in their company, since they seemed like a unit, inseparable, indistinguishable, sitting there, and also uneasy that I was so far away, surrounded by men.

A secretary came out with a batch of cloth numbers over her arm, numbered from one to fifteen. Influenced by Smithy's position at the table, she went straight to him and handed him the number one, which in fact was two number patches, joined by shoulder straps, which Smithy quickly slipped over his head, so that one number lay across his chest, the other across his back. Then she went around the table with the numbers, so that I found myself with number three. Not a bad number, I thought at the time. So there we were, sitting like football players around this rectangular table. Then fifteen officials filed in, each with a note pad and pencil, and sat around the walls, like judges at a diving contest. Each had been assigned a number, or rather two numbers. For instance, the official sitting behind me had to watch me, number three, from the back and the man opposite me, number fourteen, from the front. As far as I was concerned this whole thing was a farce. I did not necessarily want the promotion. I was content enough in my work, and I wanted above all to be left alone. But because of my work and because of my past, my role in the Mountain affair and the arrest of the family, I had been put forward as a contender for the new job. They meant it as an honor to me and it was easier for me to go along with it.

We had already been through the intelligence tests and the language ability tests and the personality tests, which I didn't mind doing at all. A little time lost in a specific task is a pleasant thing. The language test, which caused many of the others a great deal of trouble, I found soothing and absorbing. An imaginary language is postulated, and in the two hours of the test, the candidate progresses from Lesson One of the language through to Lesson Twenty, learning a new grammar, new words, nonsense syllables really, but by the end of the test, they were making sense. I was understanding them and accepting what they stood for. By Lesson Twenty, it was possible to write complete paragraphs and memos in this imaginary language and to translate whole passages.

As for the intelligence tests and the personality tests, what can I say? I just answered them honestly. Would I prefer to wash dishes in my own home by hand or in a restaurant with a dishwasher? What does a cat always have, meat, milk, fur, or purr? The tests exist and one does them. Once you catch on to the code, you are okay.

After the tests the original two hundred applying for promotion were shortlisted to fifteen. Then came the two intensive days of interviews for the one job. First, the free-for-all discussion. The chief testing official, who was a psychologist with the army, announced to us as we sat there with our numbers on, that we were to discuss a certain topic, "No holds barred," he said. We would not be held responsible for our views. The officials observing were not interested in what we were saying but only in how we said it. They only wanted to see our behavior in a discussion, he said. I knew that anyone who believed that was a fool. The topic was the Complex's political program and its role in culture. Anyone who thought the Complex and its policies were less than wonderful would be out selling peanuts on the street corner tomorrow. This was clearly a chance for the fifteen of us to show how loyal we were.

Smithy jumped straight in and fired off a list of wonderful consequences for culture caused by the Complex's political program. Someone further down, number nine I think, echoed this. Then number eight or nine, one of the women, to sound less parrot-like and to establish herself as having a point of view, which is hard considering that there is no room for individual points of view in the Complex, said, "Yes, but on the other hand perhaps work done by Complex artists qualitatively and quantitatively would be enhanced if ... " and on and on it went. I felt sorry for her. After each person said his piece he looked to Smithy.

I did not say much. I did not even nod my head in agreement. I agreed with nothing. I had nothing to say that could be said in that room. I made what could be called technical contributions. When the question of the different groups and their languages came up, I could offer something about the Mountain language and culture and the problems of translation. The observers jotted down notes. I had not realized that I was nervous, but at one point I looked down and saw my watch lying in my lap. The band had been torn apart, one of the metal links prised open. I had been fiddling with it under the table and must have broken it.

That evening there was the reception at the official residence. We still wore our numbers, now over our good clothes, and we were observed as we chatted, drank, and ate. The same observers were all around, jotting down their notes. I found myself talking with a senior official who asked me why I was so ambitious.

"Ambitious?" I asked, really surprised.

"My daughter did not even need to finish school," he said. "It isn't necessary if you have a certain standing in society. But if the Complex Leaders walked in right now, she would know how to greet them, and exactly how to behave to make them feel at ease, and she could mix them any drink they preferred. She could have them completely comfortable before calling me or whoever they had come to see." He looked around the room at the fifteen of us. "There aren't many here you could count on like that."

I found myself with a little load of used toothpicks in my hand. I had not been able to dispose of them while talking and being observed. Finally, I tucked them all behind the number on my chest, and now I can imagine the observers' notes: "Deposits toothpicks down front, ten in all."

Then, before the psychiatric interview the following day, the army psychologist took me aside and whispered, "Don't mention your father and mother. There's no need for anyone to know that." This was stupid advice, since it is clear that in all their information collecting about the candidates, everyone has collected that piece of information about me. I could just as easily stand up and say, "Don't forget about my parents, they resisted, somewhat."

The psychiatrist questioned me at length.

"What about your father?" he asked, first question.

"Dead," I answered.

"How?"

"Accident," I answered. "Car."

"Are you sure it wasn't a planned accident?"

"It was an accident," I said.

"You don't know much about them, do you?" he said.

I shrugged.

"Have you ever thought of doing the same thing?" he asked.

"Having a car accident? Never."

He spoke with me for an hour and a half, although only forty-five minutes had been scheduled. And then he asked that I be sent back for a further interview the following day. Perhaps it was because he doubted my mental state and needed to make sure. I had heard that they called you back if they were unsure, and sometimes they brought you before a panel of eight psychiatrists, which I actually would not have minded. I think I would have enjoyed eight psychiatrists in a semicircle around me listening to what I had to say. But I was getting the impression that the psychiatrist who asked me back liked me and liked hearing my voice, that he found me gratifying in some way.

After all that, I got the job. I write position papers and speeches for Wils, and I am on my way up.

I have been given a new office and a higher rank. I no longer share with the wretched Serena. I have the writers' conference, WRICOCO TWO, in a couple of weeks and the Peninsula tour coming up. And Serena still worries me. She still keeps track of me constantly.

I have a new desk and three windows to myself. I hope it means an end to the hurting legs and the dreams. As soon as people come into my office they count the windows and show a certain amount of respect. I have four writers working for me. One has two windows, two share an office with three windows, and one, a trainee, is in an office with no windows at all. I have a fine view of the river and several new Complex buildings.

I have been given permission to interview Barm and to translate his novel *Corrosion*. I cannot believe it. He has been in my mind so much. Wils's office had to approve the proposal, which is to do a series of monographs on our artists along with translations of their work to facilitate international understanding. And there is time for me to see him before the conference. I have this secret idea that Barm is the chief resister and I want to reach him.

From my side window I can see two men repairing the terrace of a tall building opposite, one of the new ones built hurriedly for GASTRO which now seem to need repairing all the time. The men are resurfacing the terrace. The fence around the terrace is waist high. It is a metal railing, embedded in a brick base which forms a little ledge. One of the men climbs onto the little ledge, to get his feet off the terrace. He throws one leg over the metal railing and straddles it, twelve stories up. And he leans his body out from the balcony, cups his hands to his mouth, and shouts to a workmate down on the ground to bring up some coffee. I am so afraid he will fall. All the sensations I would feel if I were straddling the railing of a balcony twelve stories up and leaning out over nothing I am feeling at this moment, and I feel I am going to fall off my chair, all the way to the ground. I look away, and when I look back, the men have disappeared from the terrace.

Wils, Minister of Information, gave an official barbecue to foster goodwill among his department employees. I did not want to go. But with Serena hanging around ready to escort me, and the office van ordered to come and pick us all up, there was no way to avoid it.

I had no idea what to wear. Barbecue and official seemed like a contradiction in terms. Barbecue means sandals and easy clothes, official means ceremonial clothes, the opposite. I wore sandals with heels and stockings, since bare toes seemed a little impertinent, and who am I to make a spectacle of myself or take a moral stand on the matter of dress? I just wanted to go, blend in, and get out again as quickly as possible. I wore long trousers, loose, but silky, not cotton.

"You can't go like that," Serena said when she came and stood in my doorway, open to the elements as usual. She had on pumps, and what could be called her good office clothes as opposed to ordinary office clothes.

"It's a barbecue," I said. "This, Serena, is the modern world. It has reached our Complex."

"But not with Ministers. You can see your toes. You'll be demoted."

"Okay with me," I said.

The van was sounding its horn. I led the way downstairs feeling, I might add, uneasy. My toes felt as big as sausages in their transparent skin and in the van I found myself curling them under, trying to tuck them out of sight under the brown strap of my sandal, and then the whole thing, sandal, toes and foot, under my blue trousers. But while it was possible to sit like that, I could not keep it up when we alighted.

We arrived at the Minister's mansion, Wils's new home, and made our way past the guards into the park that serves as Wils's backyard. The deer that usually prance around there had disappeared into the trees, replaced by the Information hundreds. (I have heard that Wils, good man, has discontinued the practice of previous Ministers, who sent servants among the trees to drive the deer back onto the open lawn to enhance the party scene.)

Wils came forward graciously to greet us. He was wearing faded jeans from abroad, an open-necked shirt, and tennis shoes with no socks. I thought that was hilarious. "Tell Wils he's underdressed," I whispered to Serena.

Looking around I saw that the higher the rank of the person, the more casually he was dressed. Men who normally wore handmade woolen suits to work were stepping carefully on the grass in loafers and imported sneakers and, since most of them did not own anything resembling faded jeans, the most ordinary trousers and shirts they could find. Some had found trousers patterned in bright checks and plaids. People of lower rank were dressed for an evening at the theater, having understandably agonized over the proper dress for a barbecue, a very recent innovation in the Complex. And they were sweltering in the afternoon sun. The ones who traveled abroad a lot knew that it was now a sign of true rank in certain admired countries to wear work clothes. In fact, a couple of foreign ambassadors there looked as if they had come straight from working on the railroad or running around the lake. I have never traveled abroad, but I have read and picked up a great deal.

Serena looked very cross at the sight of these dignitaries in work clothes. As she shook hands with Wils, murmuring, "Lolico," I did expect her to upbraid him for his appearance, but she stayed silent. At least Serena is held in check by self-interest and political ambition, sometimes.

The foreigners tended to stick together, talking in the shade of the trees at the edge of the lawn. Wils went to talk to a couple of journalists. I stood nearby, alone, just watching, holding my glass, thinking I would remove my stockings at the first opportunity. Then Wils came up to me, leading one of the foreign journalists.

Wils introduced us, describing me as one of the Complex's most talented young officials destined for greater things. Then he said to me, "Our friend here has some questions which I thought you could answer. Tell him what you know. Ask some questions yourself." And off he went.

The journalist was an attractive young man. His paper was prestigious in his own country, land of the colored sneaker, and abroad. He started right in with his questions, while I was still admiring his face and his springy look. I had watched him walk across the grass to me and I liked the way he moved. Very much.

"What about the Island?" he asked.

"What island?" I replied.

He looked impatient. I wanted to please him, no doubt about that, but I knew nothing of an island.

"There's an island they're sending political prisoners to, off the coast somewhere, and I'm trying to find out about it."

And then I knew that he knew things that I needed to know. I had known that people were being sent off somewhere, to jails in other towns and villages, I had thought, but I had not known about an island. I had also forgotten how inhuman journalists are, in that their biggest thrill is to get their story and use whoever they need on the way. And I was wondering why Wils had set this man on to me. I imagined Wils thought that I was stupid and that my ignorance would protect the Complex.

"It's hard for us to know what is happening here," I said. "Please tell me what you know, and I'll try to help."

"There are thousands there, and I've heard it's the worst piece of ground on this earth. But none of you will tell me anything."

I had to touch this beautiful man who was telling me these things I needed to know. I rested my hand on his arm and leaned forward and said, "I'd tell you if I knew. I know they have been sending people off, but we don't know where. I have lost several people, a whole family, that way, I think. And possibly my parents."

I could feel that this man had decided I was useless. His arm felt like the arm of a chair. There was no response at all, not a shifting of the weight on his feet toward me, not even a second look into my face to see what I was up to. He was looking over my shoulder, the way people do at parties, to see which ambassador was talking to which official.

"Thanks," he suddenly said, and took his arm back, then raced off across the lawn to a little group of major democratic allies. He could have learned a lot from me if he had bothered to listen. I could have told him about the Mountain trip, the disappearance of Lak and the family. A good feature story, good evidence of the kind of thing that is going on. But he was closed to all that. He did not even see me as a woman.

I am still going to have to do the job alone, finding Lak and the others.

Wils came back to me. "Learn anything?" he asked, smiling at me. I'm getting along well with Wils these days. I feel like a hypocrite. But what else can I do?

"What about the Island?" I asked. "Where is it?"

"He told you about that, did he?" said Wils, clicking his tongue in mild disapproval, and off he wafted again, with a little laugh.

And this morning another letter from Lak. A real love letter. The language is much better.

> My sweet one, I had a good idea of how I would miss you, but I had no real sense of the intensity of the feelings that make me spend most of my days recalling our times together and remembering especially your voice. In my mind I compose lists of words I want you to say when we're together next. I say your name, and I find that saying your name somehow, by itself, explains everything. This is necessarily brief, and I regret that because I have at the moment an almost absolute sense of your presence. This comes with my best thoughts and with love. Lak.

And I am always saying his name, too.

Then, with the next messenger round, another letter.

> . . . I want you to know that our times together were extraordinary and special for me. Whenever I was waiting for you to come, it often seemed that you might not make it. Then you always appeared from a surprising direction. You often surprised me, took my breath away, transformed moments entirely into something which

they never seemed to promise. What I most want to say is that I take our talks in the most serious way possible, and at the same time I don't feel either anxiety or despair. Among other things, our time together provided me with a new sense of what it means to understand another person. I would thank you for that, but I think the learning came from the two of us together. I catch myself with a smile on my serious face, and I know that I've been thinking of you again. It happens often. Lak.

I have been reading those letters over and over, and I am smiling, too. I read his first letter again, and can only guess that the mountains and the sea breeze he talked about mean the Island and that the family is imprisoned there, while Lak may or may not be.

Barm was sitting on the floor cutting up newspapers and filing them when I arrived. "For my historiography of the movement," he told me later. I noted how carefully he spoke. He did not say which movement, and to be doing it so openly is meant to imply that it is the Complex movement that he is documenting and that it is a loyal act.

On the walls were charts that stretched from the ceiling to the floor. Everywhere were piles of newspapers. One of his children, a little girl, was playing among the clippings. When I came in, his wife hurried in from the back and removed the child, the way a props man picks up things from Act One that are not needed in Act Two, and puts them in their place ready for the next performance.

Barm stood up and greeted me. He said good morning rather than Lolico. I was delighted. "Good morning," I replied, and that made him look at me closely.

"Please sit down," he said, and then he went and stood at the other side of the room fidgeting.

Barm comes from a Fielder family. I loved him already because of that, because he came from somewhere else, an alien in the Complex. He does not have the cosmopolitan behavior that has become admired in the Complex these days. He does not have the suaveness of Wils, or the humorless wiliness and ambition of Serena. And his language is straightforward. None of this, "You may want to be seated," and so on.

It gives a strength to his writing that is unique here. Most writers, who generally come from high Complex families, strive to imitate the masters from elsewhere, which gives their already stilted Complex language a peculiar deadness.

I was so afraid that Barm would think me stupid that I had a list of questions prepared. Yet there he was standing before me fidgeting, nervous. This is the man who wrote those novels under his bunk in jail and who, I learned, had shared a dungeon with murderers.

My questions went something like this, and luckily I did not get to ask many of them:

What languages do you prefer to write in?

What languages do you know?

Why have you written no novels in ten years?

Who do you consider the greatest writer of the Complex and its territories?

Do you consider yourself a Complex writer or a Field writer?

And so on. I would not have asked them as abruptly as that. I would have worked my way to them gently. Just the same, they were dull and obtuse, and I should have known better than to formulate them. What I really wanted to ask was, "Are you the chief resister? When did you turn against the old revolutionaries, who are now the Complex rulers, and join the new resisters? Are you all right, in good health? Can I help you?"

He seemed frightened and cantankerous. His wife came out with a tray and glasses and a pitcher. She and I smiled tentatively at each other. We did not speak, and Barm did not introduce us. Her eyes were large and darted about taking things in, scanning. Barm went and looked out the door at the yard and the lane, turning his back to us, while she deposited the tray and scurried off. Barm turned back to me. He was now standing in front of one of his charts with red ribbons and arrows, like a lineage or family tree. Two of the ribbons came out behind the top of his head, making him look like an anxious devil.

I started with my questions and he stood there answering, as if it were an exam. It was awful. The drinks stood untouched on the little table between us. The questions made him more nervous. The people passing by looked in to see who was visiting this man, and if they could not see clearly, they peered a little or moved so that they could get a good look at me from head to toe.

Before I could get past the third question, Barm suddenly started rattling things off. "See, I am making a chart of the historiography of the movement, gathering material for a modern history, including primary sources." And he pointed at his newspapers all over the place. "My latest book, not yet published, is about the national struggle, three generations, two volumes." He took a breath. "I am now more interested in history than in literature. My novels were written when I was a child, and only this last unpublished work is mature. When you're young, you don't know anything, you don't study your problems, just as long as you write, anything at all, you don't care."

"When did you stop feeling like a child?" I asked.

"I will consider myself adult after forty. However, note well that the only book of mine that has been banned is a history of the ethnic groups. I did not agree with the Complex's steps against the ethnic groups. Struggle must be violent. There is no independence without revolution. You don't bargain with your oppressors for independence. You take it. You have to fight for what you want."

He paused again for breath. There was now a row of seven or eight faces lined up outside, looking over the fence and into the room, making no effort to pretend they were not staring at me, although fortunately they could not hear what Barm was saying as he stood there.

"I have withdrawn from all political activities, however, and I am working at home. I am passionately interested in the history of the movement and in analyzing the present situation. I was a revolutionary in the old days, but I am no longer active. Nobody influenced me. I just became convinced it was the only way. All my life I have felt pressed, squeezed from every direction, and I have wondered why. I then came to see it was because I was pressed by outsiders, others, foreigners, aliens. All that foreign investment in my Field village, for instance, only made the village poorer, not richer. My whole family disapproves of the course I have taken. My father was sentenced to death by the revolutionaries for not turning against the old regime, and I myself hated them at first, when I was a boy. Then I joined them. Now I see that the present leaders, ex-revolutionaries, used the revolution to get control of things for themselves, for their own interests, and to wipe out the sincere revolutionary groups, the ones they did not like. After they were firmly in control they jailed me, and I was put in a cell alongside murderers. My hair turned white in nine months, look." And he ran his fingers through his hair, making it stand up. It was indeed white. Thick, bright, white. "That was three years ago, and I am only thirty-eight now."

I looked to the back of the room and saw Barm's wife standing in the doorway, holding their little girl. She was looking at me to see what was happening in this house, what I was intending to do.

I said to her, "Barm's writing, although he no longer values it himself, has sustained me through many difficult times, including the present." Then I said to Barm, "Are you the chief resister?" It is still hard for me to believe that I said that, straight out.

Barm laughed, and suddenly relaxed. The people outside who had been standing staring and looking very stern, also broke into smiles and shifted their positions when they saw him laugh. They could hear nothing. A woman who had held her baby on one hip changed it to the other hip. Barm came and sat down opposite me and drank a glass of syrup all at once. He laughed again, as if I had told a funny, funny joke.

"Remember," he said, "there's no such thing as a good king."

Then he leaned back in his chair. I could not quite understand what had happened.

"Tell me," he said, "why are you translating my *Corrosion*? It was an exercise, only practice at writing. I wrote it as I made my world tour. It is flimsy, I knew nothing, I was a child, and the writing itself is corroded. Why that one?"

"I like it," I said. "Also it is short and I only have a few months for the project. And I have personal reasons. I myself have always felt hypocritical. My behavior changes according to each person or group I am with. My opinions, too. I seem to have no strong convictions. I often feel that principles change to suit the situation, that we act first no matter how immorally, and find justifying principles afterwards. Perhaps everyone is like this, seeing others only in relation to himself and his own life story, never in their own context. *Corrosion* shows what happens when this is widespread. It shows how we dry up."

Barm smiled. "It is the work of a corroded author," he said. "I was allowing myself to be courted by the Complex at the time, after the victory over the old regime. My writing was at its best and strongest while I was in prison the first time and immediately after I was released, after the revolution succeeded. Then I was not corroded at all. If they ever jail me again, they should not let me have pencil and paper. In jail you can't look out so you look in. And they should never release me. It is too invigorating. When I got out of prison the first time I felt so energetic I could have exploded, like a volcano. I wrote and wrote. My children were born and they brought me new life. I felt alive. I know that my writing has deteriorated, and I have stopped writing altogether. But all my writing is bad really, though some of it less so. I was very proud of my *Stories from the*

Field when it was first published. Look, a child from the Field, uneducated, has written a book, two books, then more. Scholars befriended me. I was compared to Hemingway and Whitman. I, who cannot read Hemingway and Whitman in their original language. Now I see that *Stories from the Field* is of no value."

A policeman on local patrol had stopped outside and was dispersing the spectators. Barm sighed and stood up and went to the door.

"Good morning," he said. I wished he had said Lolico, for his own safety. "Come in and join us," said Barm.

The policeman came in. Now I would be questioned and I did not want to have to answer questions. The policeman smiled and nodded at me. I did not say anything. I did not want to say a plain good morning, in case it was used against Barm and me later. I did not want to say Lolico, because it would remind the policeman that Barm had not said it. I smiled.

"A student," Barm said of me, "of my old writing, which I would burn if I could. Make a note of that, brother. The future of the Complex is all that matters. I was saying that I used to feel inferior, a real idiot, because I knew no foreign language the way the educated leaders did. I was not sent away to school. I went to the village school and had to leave to help my father." Barm invited the policeman to sit down. "Do you know, I once met with the publisher of the largest publishing house in the Complex? I was just out of jail the first time. He asked me what I had read recently. It was a panel at the First Writers of the Complex Conference. WRICOCO ONE, remember?" I had been too young at the time, but of course I had read about it. Barm went on. "I said I had just read *Huckleberry Finn*, and Lamb's *Tales from Shakespeare*, and *The Bluebird*. That is the truth. I was reading foreign literature for the first time. And the publisher, who was mediating, laughed at me, really ridiculed me in front of an audience. 'No French authors?' he asked. 'In translation only,' I said, lying. Not only could I not read French, but I had not at that point even read French authors in translation. 'The whole of Europe is fifty years behind France,' he said, and then, as if he were trotting out every fine fact he knew, he said, 'Besides, it is Petrarch and not Dante, as is commonly believed, who is the main literary feature of the Renaissance.' "

The policeman nodded and smiled again. "Brother, I'll be on my way."

"I tell you," said Barm, detaining him, "I almost went right back to the Field. My writing has been called primitive, you know, but they mean me, because of that Petrarch-Dante matter. The man is an ex-publisher now, and I am an ex-novelist." Barm stood in the doorway, so that the policeman could not get out. "I now consider that anyone who went abroad for so-called cultural cooperation is a traitor."

The policeman said, "I just stopped by," then he turned to me, "I did not catch your name and department."

I told him.

"Are you from near here?"

"Not far," I said. "South."

He clicked his heels and bowed slightly and Barm stepped aside so that he could leave. Barm laughed. "He'll be back this evening, as usual. He is miserable having to come here and listen to me every day. I try to put on a little show for him, and just now he seemed to be having a better time than usual."

Barm's wife was back in her doorway, still looking anxious. I think it is Barm who makes her anxious, who produces that wide-eyed look, rather than the police or me.

"I went abroad," Barm went on. "That's when I wrote *Corrosion*. I was disappointed, and unhappy, and angry at everything. I felt uneducated, uncultured, inferior. And I came back, so glad to be even in the Complex, but they put me under house arrest. After the Petrarch-Dante embarrassment, I had written my *Stories from the Field*. The stories defended the ethnic groups and their way of life. Actually it was all out of the fury I felt at that publisher. Some of the best and liveliest writing, however, was being done in local languages—some Fielder stories were wonderful. But not anymore. It's the Complex language for everyone and evermore. *Stories from the Field* was praised and won prizes and it was also an embarrassment. It went against Complex goals of unity. It had come out while I was abroad, and when I came back, house arrest. I think it was the work of that publisher. He was a terrible writer himself, so caught up with being a French intellectual that his writing came out like hard little goat droppings. Nobody acclaimed anything he wrote. But he was a good businessman and his publishing house did well. He did not publish my stories, of course. Then, as the Complex got firmer about what it wanted and did not want, off he went, too. To the Island, I heard. He no longer publishes books, and I no longer write fiction. We cancelled each other out. And I'll tell you why I don't write. First, no one wants to publish it. People are scared. Second, the writing is bad. Third, it is a luxury to write. Writers must get to know people. Writers are all bourgeois, by definition, and will never see the bourgeoisie as oppressive. They must use their strength to change the path of their own thoughts.''

Barm had been standing up and talking rapidly. He stopped suddenly. ''Anything else?'' he asked.

I did not want to go. I did not want to leave him. I had great difficulty following what he had said and sorting out what he might have meant, and I was fighting the thought that he did not know what he wanted anymore. I also found him a difficult person to be with. But I did not want to leave him. I was intoxicated by his manner, and inspired. He catches you up when he speaks, and his white hair mesmerizes.

He had a little more to say. ''There has always been a mysterious voice that keeps coming back and asking me, 'What are you and what do you want?' That voice sets my soul in turmoil. And I am still trying to answer it.''

''I have that turbulence,'' I said. ''I have lost everyone I have loved. I thought you might know something. I thought you might be able to tell me something that I should do." I was speaking softly, and looking at my hands, and again I was surprised to hear myself saying those honest words, with no caution, no second thought.

"The Complex language does not originate from the proto-Complex language as everyone wishes to believe," Barm suddenly said loudly, and I wondered why he was flying off at a tangent. I looked up. The policeman was back at the door, with another, older, policeman. Barm motioned them in. "Ah, brothers, the Complex language originated in the Complex, where it has been spoken by the local people for hundreds of years, at the same time as, perhaps even before, the so-called Protocom was developing on the Peninsula and elsewhere."

The younger policeman gave a kind of sigh and looked up at the ceiling. The older policeman asked for my card and my interview permit. He copied down the numbers and other information.

"A student and an admirer," said Barm, to explain me. And then: "The syntax and structure of Complex language are different from that of Protocom. This is proved by poems and other writings. The invaders used Protocom, not Complex language, when they came, because they wanted to keep us all in the dark and not use our own language already spoken and written and in existence. Protocom is dead now, now that the invaders have gone. The ethnic languages are withered, of course. They are useless I suppose, and Complex grows strong and lively."

It all sounded convincing but it made no sense to me. Barm looked at the police. "Long live the Complex language. Lolicolang."

"Lolicolang," I said.

"Lolicolang," the two policemen said.

"Lolicop," said Barm, raising his glass to the senior policeman.

"Lolicop," I said.

86

"Lolicop," said the younger policeman, bowing to the older one.

"You're a good fellow," said the older policeman to Barm. And off they went.

I am frightened now. I do not know if it is me or Barm they are after.

"I am a weakling, and powerless. A nothing, a local curiosity. I put on a good show for everyone," Barm said. "I used to stand for struggle and pride and courage. They do this with police checkups just to remind me to watch my step. My white hair, however, still encourages others who are dissatisfied, who want to resist and agitate. And the Complex does not like this evidence of what they did to me," and he ran his fingers through his hair again. "But I am not the chief. I am not the person you want."

He sat down. I stood up to go, and Barm stood up again to see me out.

"I think you will have to do whatever it is you have to do yourself. Trust no one. Tell no one."

I find that I am collecting poems and stories written from the point of view of someone dead. They do exist, these works, although they are not plentiful. There is a poem written from the point of view of a man who dies in a plane crash. It could be argued that he did not actually die, that the crash really stands for life itself, that it is a flashforward, that he wrote his poem as the plane went down and it was thrown clear. It does not matter. I have also found a story about a woman who plans her own murder, even to the point of selecting the murderer.

I am remembering that when I was a child, about ten, I wrote a composition about a shipwreck and had a boatload of survivors sitting in one of the dinghies waiting to be rescued. I was writing in the first person. Then the boat sank, and I had to write, "Then all was quiet where we had been." I rather liked the sound of that. When it was read aloud in class, the class's clever boy, the one who seemed to know everything, started to laugh. "How could they know it was all quiet if they had drowned?" he said. The whole class started to laugh. They had believed the whole thing and had even appeared moved as I read it to them, but now they ridiculed it, and the teacher had to call for order. I felt stupid. And angry.

After that, I was so uncertain that I felt I had to borrow images. My mother loved reading and often I asked her what she had read. "This writer is so wonderful," she told me. "He compares the sun to a grapefruit in the sky." I set my next composition on a hot day and introduced the sun as a grapefruit, which earned me praise from the teacher. But at the time I had never seen or tasted grapefruit, only heard about them.

There is a woman, Dabra, a foreigner from a democratic ally, who married a Complexer. We do not have many mixed marriages. It is always difficult for a foreigner to fit in here. This is an exotic place, and strangers see us superficially. They call our Fielders lazy, those hardworking Fielders who toil all the time, year round, with very little rest or reward. Complexers, too, are beginning to ape the foreigners and call our Fielders lazy, the way Serena does. Also, Complexers, many of whom have risen from the Field, try to distance themselves from these roots by mocking them. That is why I admire Barm so much. He did none of that, and he has paid dearly.

Dabra was unsual. She learned the Complex language and easily adopted our customs, not jarring anyone or hurting anyone's feelings. We worked together once, on translations, some years ago, just after she married her husband, who was rising rapidly in the Complex service. She was quiet and did her work very well. They both appeared to be loyal Complexers, until he was caught red-handed printing resistance leaflets on a little handpress in their house. He was arrested. Dabra was out at the time, at the market shopping, and a neighbor raced out to tell her what had happened. She apparently knew more about Complex tactics than most of us, than I at any rate, at that time. She knew that her husband would not fare well and that she wouldn't either if she were caught. She thought she could do more for everyone if she got out of the Complex and its territories entirely.

She went with her basket of vegetables straight to the airport (they found the fresh vegetables later, dumped in a rubbish bin). She was dressed in the simple Complex fashion, but she was able to rearrange her skirt, so that it looked shorter, and her hair, so that she no longer looked like a Complex woman, and she went to the diplomatic enclosure where she happened to recognize a couple of her own countrywomen, wives of diplomats, waiting to take a chartered plane to a neighboring country to shop and have their evening clothes dry cleaned. They insisted on going abroad every couple of months because they said the shops and the dry cleaning in the Complex were inferior. Dabra said she would be happy to deliver the clothes to the cleaners for them, in return for a seat on their plane, and the ladies, the diplomatic wives, although they looked down on her simple way of life and her marriage, respected her and thought that they would have more time for shopping if Dabra took care of the dry cleaning. They even offered to pay her, as if she were a servant, and she accepted, since she needed some money. If the women had realized that Dabra was running away, that her husband had been arrested a couple of hours earlier, and that she, too, was wanted, they would not have cooperated in her escape, even though they were compatriots. The allies were more anxious to have the Complex and its territories happy than to protect innocent citizens.

Dabra is brilliant, and honest. She boarded the chartered plane with the women, and so escaped. She delivered the clothes to the cleaners, as instructed, although she could easily have dumped them like the vegetables as soon as she was out of sight of the airport. Then she went to her home country's embassy. With the money she had earned she cabled friends for more money and then sat down on the embassy veranda and waited for several days until it came. She flew home, and for the last few years has worked constantly on behalf of the political prisoners of the Complex. She reads all the newspapers and clips out everything she finds about the Complex. Most articles in the press follow the official Complex line. Then Dabra checks the news stories with whatever other reliable information she can get. For instance, a resister escaping will come to her and allow himself to be interviewed as she asks question after question about the situation. Or she will go down to the docks and find a boat that has put in at the Complex during its voyage. She will talk to the captain and the sailors and ask about anything they might have heard or seen. Then she assembles a newsletter, which she sells by subscription.

I came across one of her newsletters only the other day. It had been found in someone's belongings after he was arrested at the airport on his return from abroad. The newsletter, sent to Information for analysis, was superb. And through it I have learned more about the Island. I think there must be thousands of people there.

Dabra, all that distance away, has pieced together more about the Island that I have been able to here in the Complex. I don't know how she does it, but if ever I have the opportunity, I will do whatever I can to help her.

All of Barm's books have been banned. Serena came happily into my room last night and took my copies from the shelf.

"I'm collecting for the whole dorm," she said, "but you seem to be the only one who has a substantial collection. They're to be recycled."

I wanted to fly at her and knock her to the floor. I wanted to cry. But I have found a way to stop myself crying. It is to bite the inside of my bottom lip hard so that if my face moves to cry it hurts too much, and I can keep a straight face. It works well and helps me survive these days. Also, I am increasingly in awe of the inner mechanism that keeps us, some of us, from killing, maiming, and abusing. There is an invisible barrier that stops me from doing harm to Serena. It stops me from pushing her off the terrace, and from running her down if I am driving and she is crossing the street.

Barm did say that he would be happy if his books were burned. But that was in front of the policeman. Nevertheless, I do believe that he no longer values his work.

My copy of *Stories from the Field* that has sustained me for so long has gone. My *Corrosion*. All of them. I am sick. Today I went to see Wils. We leave next week and I needed to discuss my conference speech and my assignments for the tour.

"I'm glad you got your interview with Barm in time," he said. "I hope you'll write a report for us."

"His books are banned," I said. Maybe I yelled. "And what about the project, the translation?"

Wils smiled at me and put his arm around my shoulder. "Come now, Neila. You're being childish."

"But he is nothing," I said. "He is harmless. He is a writer who no longer writes. His stories have lost their power. He has lost his strength. His powerful work was written when you were all struggling together to throw out the old regime. His struggle was yours. He is just a person, with a wife, children, and a little house. All he does is chart the national struggle, in his own house. Why couldn't you leave him alone?"

"Me?" said Wils. "What makes you think it is me? But you could let me have it all in a report."

"What for?" I said. I was about to burst into tears.

"You were one of the last to see him. It should go on record, I think. Confidential, of course."

"You mean it's not just his books? He has been sent away?"

Wils told me that Barm was being sent to the Island. He was a symbol and had to be removed for a while. Wils told me not to be naive and asked me if I thought the Complex was a child-care center or a kindergarten.

The odd thing is that Barm, personally, is difficult, not a joy to be with. Wils is a joy to be with, warm and kind. And yet

Wils is the villain, I think. Look at what he condones, although I cannot believe that he ordered Barm's arrest.

I have done it. I have given my paper at WRICOCO TWO, and I may be off to the Island as a result. Wils called me to his office afterwards and asked me what I thought I was doing. I was no longer a child, he said, and he was thinking of cancelling my appointment with the tour and sending me away to the Island for a little stay, where I could fraternize with undesirables in peace. But I think he likes me and my speechwriting too much to give it up. And I think it still has not crossed his mind that I am a real resister. He must think that I am not capable of holding a strong opinion, or taking a stand, and I think he believes that I am just an innocent. After he scolded me, he said, thoughtfully, "It doesn't really hurt the Complex, I suppose, to have a maverick in its delegation. The Complex can use it to show it is not repressive. And it is useful for us." That is sophisticated of him. But he will be sorry that he did not have me put away.

WRICOCO TWO is taking place at the conference center near the GASTRO tower. In the middle of the conference room are the tables for the press and the verbatim reporters. The benches for the delegates rise in circular tiers. The guards inspect the water jugs and glasses for poison. Art work sanctioned by the Complex adorns the walls. Writers and arts administrators from abroad have been invited.

Until this morning I was a member of the Complex delegation. From where I sat I faced a piece of moving sculpture. Ten arrows or spears of metal, hammered flat and painted red, pierce a white disc, a bullseye target that has been shattered. The piece is balanced so that one or other of the spears, and sometimes several at once, are able to move back and forth through the disc. Whenever someone opens the door and creates a mild draft, the spears move gently. The thing is called VICTOCOM, Victory of the Complex, or, I prefer to think,

Victims of the Complex.

The television cameras were set up. The interpreters were in their booths. Twenty allies had sent delegates. I was to speak on Complex Writers Today. I had been allowed to allude to Barm in connection with the revolution. My speech had been checked by Wils's office, and copies had been given to the interpreters and the press. But I had changed the speech, and I was not certain that I had the courage to stand there on the podium and read it. But the conference was being televised and filmed and broadcast to all the territories and abroad and it was possible that Lak and others and possibly Barm himself would hear it. I wanted them to take courage, to endure.

This is what I said at the conference, starting out as expected:

"To think of the Complex and its territories, COMPATER, usually means to think in terms of overwhelming success, growth, originality, and benevolence regarding economic and political development. Or else it means to think of the beauties of Paradise, the beaches, the happy people, the arts and crafts, and so on. But because of the paucity of material available to non-Compater people, to foreigners, very little is known about the Compateriots, our thinking, problems and hopes, and how these are reflected in cultural developments inside Compater today. These developments, particularly in the field of literature, are an integral part of success and growth and are the topics to which I wish to address myself today . . ."

Bland enough. Everyone in the conference room seemed to subside, settle down in their chairs to last out my predictable statement.

"I have been taking part in a project devised by the Complex to facilitate cultural exchange and understanding, within Compater and abroad. I have translated works of our various literatures into Complex language and have overseen their translation into various international languages, which is one way of implementing our aims. Complex language has grown with the Complex, the one has fertilized the other . . ."

They all looked bored out of their minds. I saw Wils look at his watch. The interpreters were sitting stolidly mouthing their words.

"I chose to translate the work of Barm, one of our most prolific, talented, and controversial writers." I loved saying controversial. None of this was in the original. I was actually enjoying the sound of my voice in the microphone, which surprised me since I am usually shaking with apprehension at anything that requires me to do anything out of the ordinary.

"Since our revolution, Barm has published novels, stories, essays, and articles. Of all our writers he is the one who writes honestly and to the point. He sees us without adornment, tells his stories simply, his language devoid of circumlocution. His words are reduced to a minimum, shorn of unnecessary affixes. He reveals, as no other writer dares, the atmosphere of the revolution, the effect, often corrupting, often tragic, on those who take part, as in *Revolutionary Family*. He describes the Fielder way of life, its language and society now almost wiped out, as in *Stories from the Field*. And he shows us our problems after success, as in *Corrosion*. There are many opinions about Barm and his work . . ."

I looked up for a moment and saw the interpreters in their booths looking down at me, then back at their texts, going through the pages to see if they were in the wrong order.

"Some language experts condemn his writing as too realistic, too blunt, lacking in style and refinement. In fact, his style and language are so strong and original that they have stimulated the growth of our Complex language."

I saw Wils frowning. His assistant leaned toward him and whispered something. Then the assistant got up and went to the door and stood beside the guards, watching first me, then the delegates and the press, then the clock.

"Traditional groups accuse Barm of lack of respect for tradition. In fact, Barm went to jail, sent there by his own Compateriots, because he wrote about the rights of an ethnic group and its traditions. The elite condemn him for being too ethnic and refusing to use great foreign literature as sources of inspiration and literary models. In fact, he looks for a truly Compateriot form of expression, so that our literature can be part of that great body of international literature. The elite say he is uneducated and simple-minded, because he does not know whether Petrarch or Dante had the greater influence on the Renaissance. In fact, he is our Petrarch and our Dante in our own Renaissance. He has not written a novel in ten years. He may never write another ..."

Wils was looking thunderous. The assistant at the door had his hand on the arm of the guard next to him. Members of the press were taking notes. Delegates were adjusting their earphones. The interpreters must have discarded their advance texts completely and been trying to keep up. I had to speak quickly now. I did not know if Wils would have me hauled off.

"Barm lived in a small house in the crowded heart of the Complex. He was writing a historiography of the struggle. He filed his collections of clippings. He supported his wife and children. He was alert, thin, smiling. During the revolution, he worked as a correspondent for the revolutionary newspaper. Then he was captured by the old regime, as they were losing, and jailed. And during that first imprisonment he wrote his best work. He was never content with his work. It was always the work in progress that would be the best. We talked about the Complex, when I visited him last week. We talked about writing, his life, his fears, and we were joined by members of the police who inspected him twice a day. I say lived, was writing, was alert, thin and smiling, because Barm no longer lives in that small house. He no longer writes that historiography of the struggle and files those clippings. Because last week he was sent to the Island, a little spot, a resort, to which we send some of our people to help them clear their heads and come back refreshed. We cannot claim credit for originating the idea of rehabilitation, but we have devised a variation that could well be of interest to others to emulate, and we shall be happy to explain it to those of you who would like to know more.

"Barm looks like an old man, and he is not yet forty. His hair is white and can remind the new generation, those who have only heard secondhand about the struggle and the revolution, of his contribution. We have gained from him far more than we can possibly give in return.

"Compateriot writers today are beset with problems. They lack money. They lack paper, and the printers also lack paper, and there is at the moment a three-year lag between acceptance and publication. And acceptance is already hard to achieve, given the criteria set by the Complex for publication. This is one of the reasons we have not seen a novel for five years from any writer. There is still a healthy potential. We are delighted that you are here and are interested in us."

I finished there because the guards had been moving forward, like racers edging forward waiting for the pistol shot. Wils did not give the order. When I sat down, Wils's seat next to mine was empty, and from the activity of the spears of VICTOCOM, I guessed he had flounced out. The conference room was seething, as they say, and several press members got up and left. I had no idea what would happen, but I felt, unreasonably, secure and elated.

What I had said in my speech was actually guarded, not revealing or revolutionary, but it is true that informed observers could interpret what I said. Afterwards, the overseas press wanted to talk to me, and before Wils could get to me, I told them that Barm was on the Island, along with thousands of others, I believed, undergoing rehabilitation, and as Wils came toward me, I said that the prisoners were living under excellent and benevolent conditions and, in fact, the Ministry would be more than happy to show the world how the Complex treats its citizens who need help directing their full efforts to the common good. I said that the Island was comfortable, efficiently run, that whole families could be out of their homes here and off to the Island for rehabilitation and a new family installed in their vacated home overnight, all carried out smoothly and with a minimum of stress for all involved.

I have been sent on an intensive four-day indoctrination at a Ministry house at the seaside. Wils made excuses for me after WRICOCO, maintaining that Mountainers and other ethnics are primitive and ill-educated and that it takes a while for them to be trained. After my public display at WRICOCO they cannot really get rid of me immediately. Besides, they need someone like me, a woman, an ethnic, young, to legitimize their image. And my odd way of talking and my odd ideas they tolerate somewhat. I am a token. Just the same, Wils wanted to teach me a lesson.

The weekend has been a combination of humiliation and luxury. A bit like the jail we visited on the way to the Mountain.

It is not good for me here. They call me an anti-Complex Complexer. They say I am defiling the past suffering of the Complexers. They make ethnic jokes and say my people speak with hot potatoes in their mouths. (Mountain people, speaking the Complex language, do take particular care to speak correctly and with flair, so as not to be ridiculed, and because of the beauty of their own language they also render the beauty that is in the Complex language. If a Mountainer did not take care with his speech, he would be accused of sounding too ethnic.) I have never been around such viciousness, and I am trying not to take it personally. I am trying to remember that this will last only a few days, but they know how to hurt.

I am still to go on the Peninsula tour, but they have assigned Serena to accompany the group. That is my punishment. She will officially be my assistant. She is pleased and angry. She likes the honor, but hates me and my success. She likes her work as Complex spy and tale-teller, but hates being an assistant to me, whom she considers ineffectual and stupid. To me, Serena is like a cancer. She is stuck to me, she recurs and erodes. She is here this weekend, having a good time gloating over my temporary fall from grace and my misery.

The tour is going well. I am cheered because I see that the resistance activity here has been by no means squashed and I feel particularly confident. I write undistinguished speeches with a minimum of anguish and behave politely at receptions. I feel as if I still have a number on my back, that I am watched by my own colleagues. But I feel that I know what I am doing, at last.

We are having several days of rest at the coastal villa belonging to one of the Peninsula dignitaries, before going back to the Complex. We sit on the grass in the shade, with the straits and the lighthouse on the point before us. I read or doze or write. Serena watches me. I wear shorts, which is slightly frowned on by the others, but Wils has said it is all right. He seems to be enjoying himself and relaxing. Now and then we all walk across the grass to the sand and go for a swim. No one can swim very well and we look lilke a group of grown-up children, tottering about at the water's edge. Often the men just roll up their trouser legs and paddle up to their ankles. I can do better than that, but I am not a strong swimmer. I can do the strokes, but I have no endurance.

The servants cook wonderful food. A military guard is deployed around the house and the perimeter of the property, just to make sure that zealous resisters do not wipe out this rather rare group. One soldier, our personal guard, sits under a nearby tree.

It is so pleasant that it is for a moment hard to believe that I am a resister and that the Complex and its territories are in the midst of a kind of war. The villa is so spacious that Serena and I have separate rooms. Strange but true. An astounding piece of good luck. Serena appealed to Wils to move her to my room, since we were the only two women and should stick together. But Wils waved her away — he clearly has never liked her much, which pleases me—and said to leave things as they were.

At night I can hear the military guard making a racket in the courtyard, singing, fooling around, and I can write to my heart's content. Because there are men present, I am allowed to shut my door.

"Why is your light on?" Serena just called to me, knocking on the door. And she turned the doorknob. But because of the men and the generally uncertain situation, I can keep the door locked. The first night here I was awakened by someone turning the doorknob, trying to get in. I heard a voice whispering something but I could not tell whose voice it was and I did not reply.

But when footsteps clomp up to my door and a voice calls out, "Why is your light on?" there is no mistaking Serena.

"Can't sleep," I say. "Too noisy downstairs," or "I'm working."

"Let me in, I'll help you," Serena says.

But I tell her she will be more useful to me after a good night's sleep. I enjoy reminding her that she is my assistant.

Once or twice, after I said I couldn't sleep, Serena called out to the soldiers from her window, telling them to stop their noise. But they responded by hooting and laughing and calling to her to come down and join them. The next morning at breakfast Serena complained to Wils.

"Make the troops stop the noise and talking at night. Neila can't sleep."

Recently I have been treated like a princess, a kind of expensive and precious piece of property. Serena watches out for my sleep. Wils is kind and solicitous.

"It really doesn't matter," I said. "Soon we'll be back in our own quiet dormitory." I dread going back, but I am always anxious, too, when I am away. I hate my room there, but I am often frightened to leave it. Every day when I get back after work, I notice that I hold my breath as I climb the stairs and walk along the back terrace to my room. I expect to find it ransacked, my things destroyed or confiscated. I imagine walking in and finding it completely occupied by a new tenant who wonders what I am doing there. There has been talk recently of my moving to a small house, one of the Ministry's, set aside for upper-level employees. I would have to share it with one other woman. And since that is sure to be Serena, I have not been overeager to follow it up.

"Wils, tell the soldiers to be quiet," Serena nagged. She seems much quieter this trip, nagging and whining instead of bellowing. A lot of the time she is surly and withdrawn. She must consider this behavior appropriate to the job of watching me. She is certainly dedicated.

Wils laughed and ruffled her hair, which made me laugh. Literal, humorless Serena with her hair messed up like a little girl.

"Men will be men," said Wils, and winked at me.

And I laughed more. Such frivolity, at breakfast, with the minister and two deputy ministers. Perhaps Wils likes the nighttime rowdiness of the troops for the same reason that I do. It makes for privacy.

Wils said he wanted to take me to visit the old palace. He had access to the private rooms and said they were magnificent and not to be missed. We happened to pass the palace after an official reception. It was three or four o'clock in the afternoon, and Wils asked the driver to stop and let us out. He told the driver to wait and said we would be back in a little while. The soldier who accompanied us everywhere heaved himself out of the car with a big sigh, ready to go with us, but Wils said he needed only to stay at the car, and the soldier sank back against the door happily. Serena and the two deputies had already gone ahead in a different car. I knew Serena would be fuming when I did not show up immediately.

Wils had the key to the palace. How he got it I have no idea. Probably from the governor of the region at lunch or something. Since it was a normal work day and the palace was a little way from the town center it was by no means crowded. A few people walked in the grounds and in the courtyards and in the public rooms downstairs. But although no one lived there now, the second floor, the private quarters, was barred by an iron gate at the bottom of a flight of stairs. Wils unlocked this and up we went. I have been feeling lighthearted on this trip. It has been fun and I am no longer constantly afraid, which is why I can sit here under the trees and write this in front of our little group. At the top of the stairs there was a long gallery with painted wooden panels on the wall, and doors at long intervals. We walked slowly along the gallery until Wils stopped in front of one of the decorated panels.

"We go in here," he said.

There was no door. I turned to him and he laughed at me. He turned me around to face the panels. He stood behind me and reached around me to take my hands in his. I felt his body against my back. Wils made my hands, my fingertips really, search the panels, up and down, until I found the catch. It was part of the elaborate design painted on the front panel that was the door, a fancy little doorknob. Because the whole panel was painted with identical handles, with the shadows also painted in, it was impossible to detect, at least at the beginning, the real handle.

Wils told me it was a secret room, historically very interesting. He had his cheek against my hair as his hand on top of my hand turned the handle. We stepped in onto soft dark carpet. Our footsteps made no sound. Wils closed the door behind us. It was dark in the inner room. I could make out a shape, an animal with shining eyes, crouched on the floor in front of me, and I drew in a breath to scream. Wils, still behind me and holding me, must have felt this and he clapped a hand over my mouth. I wondered if he intended to kill me. I was frightened again. As my eyes got used to the dark it became clear that the animal was a tiger, stuffed and positioned, as a joke I suppose, to give anyone coming into the room a fright. I tried to get Wils's arms from around me. At first, feeling him touch me as I had searched for the door handle, I had wanted his arms to stay there. I thought of Lak. But the tiger jolted me and made me remember that Wils was the enemy. I turned to him, or rather he turned me to him, keeping his arms tightly around me, and he kissed me. I suppose I should have guessed that Wils had been planning something like this—the job, the allowances made for my transgressions, the doorknob to my room turning in the night, and so on. And I have to admit that I have been flattered by his attentions and by his obvious satisfaction at my work. It is particularly odd, since I was hardly aware of him on that first trip we made to the Mountain so many months ago. I have also enjoyed Serena's jealousy.

There we were, Wils kissing me and holding me very tightly so that I could not get away, and beginning to make love to me, and I frightened and also aware that I was wanting to be made love to, actually wanting the Minister of Information to seduce me, in a secret room in a practically deserted palace with rugs and a stuffed tiger. Wils stopped kissing me and held my face in his hands and looked at me.

"I have been waiting a long time for this," he said.

I began to cry. I put my head on his shoulder and cried. Then I looked up over his shoulder and I saw another couple across the room.

"Wils, there's someone here—" but as I spoke I saw in the gloom that it was Wils and I, reflected in a huge mirror, and that mirrored panels completely covered the four walls of the room and the ceiling. I stepped back from Wils to look around. The mirrors made it difficult to see where the corners of the room were, where the ceiling met the walls, and I could not see where the doors were, not even the door by which we had come in. There were no windows that I could make out, unless they were covered by mirrored shutters. Wils had not let go of me. I stood back from him a little, looking around, but he kept his hands on my shoulders. Then I saw the tiger, crouched, and thought that I could always use it as a guide to get out, since it faced the doorway.

Apart from being excited by Wils, I was also excited to be away from other people. No Serena, no guard, no servants. I did not want Wils to stop. I looked at his face. It is still amazing to me that he has such a pleasant face and kind voice, and yet is a tyrant, mad perhaps, who can have people transported to the Island, a penal colony, for nothing. I could feel he was strong from his arms and hands, and that was also a surprise to me. He kissed me again. One hand slid up over my shoulders to hold the back of my head, so that I felt totally inside his grasp. And we lay down on the carpet beside the stuffed tiger and made love as if we had hours and hours to ourselves, as if there were no soldier with a rifle leaning against the car outside, no chauffeur, no casual visitors downstairs looking at the relics, no official Peninsula tour. Then we lay there on the carpet, me in Wils's arms, my head against his chest, and his lips telling me through my hair that he loved me. The tiger had been knocked off its course, forty-five, ninety degrees, I have no idea, and it lay on its side.

Wils started to get dressed again. He sat me up and helped me dress, kissing my shoulders, my hair, and my hands.

"Look at your face," he said, and led me up to the wall to see my bright red cheeks. And he stood behind me and told me again, as we looked at ourselves in the mirror, that he loved me.

"How will we get out?" I asked. "Where's the door?" I started going around the walls looking for the way out, for any door at all.

Wils laughed and said I panicked too easily, but then he could not find the door either. And we both went round and round the walls looking for a latch. Wils looked worried.

"Set the place in order," he said, which only meant picking up the tiger and straightening some rugs. We combed our hair and tucked ourselves in neatly. My cheeks were less red, and we looked our immaculate official selves again. But we could not get out.

In that chamber our voices and movements were muffled

and no sound at all penetrated from the outside. Even if we had vanted to, we could not bang on the walls to try to attract attention without breaking the priceless mirrors.

"What if it's the enemy?" said Wils. "What if they knew we were coming here? They could get rid of us and effectively destroy our work." Wils was trying to figure out what to do. I was not afraid of the resisters. If a new insurgency started, fine. But I was worried that we would be found and I did not want anyone, meaning Serena, to have any concrete evidence against us. I could see her notes back to the Secret Service: "The Minister and the subject spent several hours in a secret palace room alone. When found, their cheeks were somewhat rosy."

We went around the walls once more, placing the tiger at the panel where we began and running our fingers carefully along each seam, each join in each mirror. We could not reach to the ceiling, and there was nothing to stand on, although who would want to put the catch to a door up near the ceiling? A king who wanted to drive his women crazy, I suppose, by keeping them prisoner in a mirror cage.

I imagined us dying there in that secret room, sandwiched, soundproofed and hidden, between the other palace rooms, and lying undiscovered for years.

As we were going along one wall I heard a vague sound, voices, and we deduced that that must be the wall that gave onto the gallery. So we concentrated on those panels. Then we heard tapping and shouting, very dim. Later I learned that the soldier had got worried and come looking for us, but when he tried to get through the gate at the foot of the stairs and began rattling it, the caretaker had come running and yelling, telling him it was not open to the public.

I told Wils to hold me on his shoulders. It was hard for me to get up there. I climbed up Wils as if he were a tree, one foot on his knee, then one on his hip, hoisting myself up while Wils tottered and braced himself against the mirror. Then once I was up it was hard for me to keep my balance and hard for Wils to bear my weight. He grunted and took little steps as I felt along the joins of the mirrors right up to the ceiling. I found the catch. We were going to rush out into the light and air, but the soldier was passing by with the caretaker who, although he had opened the gate for the soldier finally, was still telling him that the upstairs quarters were closed. We held the door shut, until they passed. Then we found we had locked it again, and I had to climb up on Wils once more to release the catch. We straightened our clothes. Wils gave me a kiss. Then we rushed out of the room. The door closed behind us and we ran down the stairs and through the gate, and pretended to walk calmly back to the car, where we were waiting when the soldier came back.

"You kept us waiting," Wils said to him. "I told you to stay with the car, not to go off like a tourist looking at relics."

"I thought you might be in trouble," the soldier said. "There are resisters around, remember," and he sulked all the way back, while Wils and I sat in the back seat, giggling a bit at our good fortune at being free. I moved slightly closer to him and sat back, with my head against the leather headrest and my eyes closed.

I am sitting here in the open air under the trees writing, allegedly, various reports and a speech for Wils to give on our return to the Complex, entitled "Old and New on the Peninsula Today." There is so much space on the grass that it would be too crass, even for Serena, to stand or sit right next to me to see what I am writing. While we all know that Serena is here to watch me, it is not official or openly acknowledged, and she also has to act as my assistant. I try to keep her very busy, and I have given her some pages of the speech and a report to type while I write what I please. This place is wonderful. I am still the only one wearing shorts and with bare feet. The others cannot forget their rank and are in trousers, ironed shirts, shoes and socks as if they were going to a funeral. But they have at least taken off their coats. Serena wears a full skirt and two petticoats. I keep a skirt beside me, because Wils has said that Peninsula officials are likely to drop by today and he also does not like the military guards to see me in shorts when they make their rounds late in the afternoon, although Wils himself is obviously enjoying the sight of me, and I am enjoying his enjoyment. Wils and one deputy minister are playing checkers in the shade. The other deputy minister is walking up and down the beach, thinking.

I think that this is what I will have Wils say when we get back. He will make the statement from the airport:

"What is the average age Complex boys and girls marry? What do Complex people think of the Peninsula? It was hard to believe that the eager and well-mannered young Peninsula students who asked these enthusiastic questions one peaceful Sunday morning belonged to the same generation as the shouting demonstrators who had the day before marched through the main Peninsula town and even blocked our own procession as they called for a general strike.

"This is one aspect of the diversity that is a constant feature of daily life on the Peninsula—indeed in the whole of the Complex and its territories. In the space of two days I attended the opening of an art exhibition, the meeting of a traditional literary club, and Heroine Day celebrations. I visited a hospital, inspected a new hospital under construction, and was present at the demonstration by striking workers. And all this is an area with only one million inhabitants. The Peninsula still basks in glory as the former revolutionary capital of the new Compater nation, when it was the center of revolutionary activities against the old regime.

"Today, the Special Area of the Peninsula, as it is termed, still inspires our younger generation. The morning of the demonstration we were in a Jeep, making a tour. We tried to size up the situation."

I am hoping that Wils will accept the mention of the strike and the anti-Complex demonstration. After all, everyone knows that the unrest is the reason our little party is making this tour. And I have been telling him that it is better in the long run to tell the truth about things, to be straightforward. But my own aim is to have the activities of the resisters mentioned as much as possible, to get them as much coverage as possible, to show people that resisters and protesters are alive and active and are real human beings themselves, who walk and laugh and talk.

Serena has come out with some typed pages and has picked up the next batch to take back in. She has set up her typewriter in a little room that is just off the front veranda. She can see us from where she types, and she is wearing a sly look on her face, as if she is enjoying seeing me make another blunder with this speech, similar to the WRICOCO TWO affair. She is probably delighted at the thought that I will be put away somewhere for sure this time. But I am feeling terrific, and Serena waits while I finish the piece:

''The demonstrators were mainly young people, smiling and shouting and jostling each other, as if they were going to a picnic. They were led by serious older students and workers, possibly resistance leaders. Besides demonstrating against the high price of books, tuition fees, and inefficient food distribution, they wanted the Complex official responsible for sending Complex advisers to the Peninsula to be sacked, and they wanted the building of the new Complex office block halted until the pay of the workers is raised. They accused the official and the Complex in general of acting contrary to the ideals of the original revolution and struggle, which forbade ethnic exploitation and domination of one group over another. We followed five hundred young people and their slogans, as they sang to the tune of 'Oh my darling' words to the effect that we should go home. They waved their signs at us, laughing and accusing us of being corroded. In the villages we were accused in the same friendly fashion. Meanwhile, vendors peddled assorted wares and wondered when prices would come down, and traditional dramas echoed across the square. This contrast between the new and the old, the changing and the static, modern and traditional, can be seen in every aspect of daily life on the Peninsula today.

And it is our strength."

I write the word SQUARES at the top of each page, for fun, to tease Serena.

"What's SQUARES?" she finally asked.

"Oh, Serena, shame on you. Squash the resisters, of course," I said.

"Hear, hear," said one of the deputies.

Wils gave me a fond smile. "We'll have to have you writing our official slogans when we get back," he said.

Just then the deputy who had been walking on the beach came across a large rowboat on the sand and called to us to come for a row. Such spontaneity. I have graciously, in a fit of unwarranted good will toward Serena, told her to leave the typing until later and go for a row. Wils and the deputy playing with him are stopping their checkers in mid-game. Wils has written a note which he puts next to the board: "Do not touch this game."

"Come on, Neila," he calls, and I think I will join them. The soldier with his rifle is getting to his feet and it looks as if he will have to come, too. There is room for six in the old tub. What a lark.

PART III: ISLAND

Now that I am out of the hospital, I have to sit and write again. It is difficult to start again. I have forgotten the mood, the reasons I am doing this. But if I do it scene by scene, episode by episode, one step at a time, everything will come together.

I have been falling asleep, not just unobtrusively in a crowd or sitting alone, but when someone is talking directly to me. I was at a reception sitting on a couch against the wall. A young woman was talking to me, and while she was asking me something I dozed off. Then when my head fell forward I woke up. She was still talking. Last night, when I myself was talking, sitting down, telling about something that had happened on the Peninsula, not the accident, something lighter, perhaps the demonstration, I fell asleep in the middle of my own sentence. I woke up almost at once, with the feel of the word still in my mouth. Perhaps we had been arguing about nonexistent problems.

On my last day in the hospital they came to tell me I was now Acting Minister. They are looking for someone more senior, but I will do for the time being because I have a certain reputation and because I know Wils's policies and can continue them for a while.

I am still exhausted from recent events and from one week on the job. I now use Wils's office, a corner office with four windows on one wall, two on the other, a carpet, and a sofa. On my first day the spokesman came and said that members of the press were asking about the Island visit I had promised at WRICOCO TWO.

I had forgotten about it. I have only been back from the Peninsula two weeks and I have not been able to think too clearly. But on the spur of the moment I said, "Arrange a boat and accommodation on the Island for as many as want to go."

The spokesman thinks I am crazy, but my reputation for erratic originality lets me get away with such things. Wils's assistant, who is now my assistant, nodded at the spokesman to show him that he agreed with me, that what I say is to be taken seriously. A blissful change from Serena. Fortunately the assistant, who admired Wils enormously, remembers that Wils held me in great esteem and had been training me. Now that I am Minister, Acting Minister rather, he sees it as a mandate from Wils, and he stands by me, in much the same way that Wils stood by me during those various transgressions of mine. Poor Wils. He imparted principles in spite of himself. But I do not know how much longer I can get away with all this. I have asked the assistant to bring me a list of the people who are thought to be on the Island. I have discovered that no one knows for sure just who is there. He is putting together a master list from all the sources he can find — the Justice Ministry, Immigration, Police, the Armed Forces, and, most oddly, Tourism and Education. Estimates vary from three thousand to ten thousand, but no one can say whether these figures include families sent with the exiles and children born on the Island. I have told the assistant to keep the list top secret for the moment. I want to use it as effectively as I can and quickly.

I have my first press conference tomorrow and I am excited and terrified. I am getting a lot of attention because of my age and because I am a woman and because I have been involved in unusual and even spectacular developments. They will ask me about the Island, and they will ask me about the Peninsula and what happened. And I am going to tell the truth, which is simple, but I shall omit the visit to the palace and what happened between Wils and me, which really concerned only us.

I was interrogated in the hospital by Justice. I still dream that

I am walking knee-deep on a narrow sandbank in the water. There has been some kind of catastrophe, and there are dead bodies all around. Some are underneath the water on the sand, some floating. Others are not quite dead yet and are struggling to get out of the water. But it is hopeless. Some of them reach out to me. I cannot help them because I am not strong enough. The current is swift and I am having great difficulty keeping my balance and holding to my course. If I step off this sand bar out of my depth to save one person, they will all grab at me and we will all drown. What can I do? I can't help them. I can't. I walk with my arms out, as if I am on a tightrope. A man is waiting for me at the shore — I believe it is Lak standing there with his arms stretched out to me, urging me to try hard, to concentrate, to reach him. It is terrible to struggle through the water and see them all dying. They call out to me with their last breath. But what can I do? I can't help them. They call out to me, and I can't help them. I try to attract the attention of rescue helicopters. One man, in a diver's suit, tries to get out of the water, to clamber onto my sandbank. His suit weighs him down. His oxygen has run out. I see him fall under the water, dragged down by his suit. He surfaces, then goes under. It is clear he knows he cannot be saved. I point to him, hoping to direct someone's attention to him. He surfaces and takes off his helmet, struggling to get it off so that he can drown naturally, peacefully, not cut off from the water, his grave, by his suit and helmet. Then he goes under. I step carefully over arms and legs, parts of drowned bodies that have drifted onto the sandbank, but I do not seem to be getting closer to the man on the shore. From the beach it must look as if I am walking on the water, in the bright sun, almost on top of the beautiful blue water, having a wonderful lark, just walking across the water to Lak.

When the six of us got into the rowboat that day it was a lark. I wanted the tour to go on and on, even though I had not forgotten my mission and the several thousand people, detained unjustly, whom I had to save. Since the palace, Wils had been coming to my room at night and we made love as often as we could. I was very happy, to be held and loved and to give something to Wils. Although Wils was so much older than I, he seemed to have the same need. But when we made love it was Lak I was touching and talking to. For the first time in years I was not thinking what next, what does this really mean.

Serena must have guessed what was happening but she could not do anything about it, at least not while we were on the tour. She must have been furious. She usually alternated from boisterous and guffawing to surly and misanthropic, and those last days she became unfailingly surly and more clumsy than usual, spilling her glass of water, dropping things. She did not seem to be able to stand anyone talking to anyone else at all. If Wils and I talked at the table, she spilled hot coffee on herself. She had taken to wearing her sunglasses at all hours, indoors and out. They wrapped around her face, and secretly, in bed, Wils and I called her Fly's Eyes. Her glasses gave her the appearance of being able to see to the front and the sides all at once.

When I magnanimously said, "Serena, type later, go for a row now," she said, "No thanks, I have to write a report." Then I practically ordered her to go for a row. "Type later," I said.

I sometimes did not like to let Serena out of my sight, either. I knew she was out to wreck everything she could. I thought that I would stay behind while everyone else rowed. I wanted some time to myself with Serena safely stuck in the little boat out in the straits, but when Wils called for me to come it seemed like a wonderful thing to do. So I put on my sunglasses and joined them. The men in their polished black shoes looked silly clambering into the boat. A what's-wrong-with-this-picture tableau. Serena did not take off her shoes, either, but bunched up her skirt and petticoats and sat like a lump at the bow. I found myself giving orders, perhaps because I was by far the most agile in shorts and bare feet. The two deputies were at the oars. The soldier was splashing unnecessarily ankle-deep in water at the side of the boat, as if it were dry land. The water must have got into his boots but he did not seem to notice. His rifle was slung across his back, luckily he had no bayonet, because everyone had to duck as he slung himself over the side of the boat and rolled in, his rifle barrel sweeping through the air. This, I thought, no one would believe. The boat rocked and everyone held on while the soldier got himself upright and sat in the bow next to Serena, his feet dripping water. He just sat there. Part of the job. I was holding the boat steady and waiting to push it off and jump in.

I was still pondering what Wils had said as we walked across the sand to the boat. "You're writing too much. It's good for you to put down your work sometimes. The speeches can't be taking that much time. You're too involved in writing things down. Don't do it. I'm trying to warn you." I was already thinking, he knows, he has known all the time what I am doing, that I am a resister. Then he said, "Forget trying to be like Barm and those activists. People like him end up on the Island. Forget him. You would do better to emulate me. Try to be like me, and you will survive."

It dawned on me that this man, this man with the strong hands and gentle voice who had been telling me that he loved me, was threatening me. He could have me arrested. It seems I have to be hit on the head before I believe that there are falling rocks. Wils was jealous of Barm, was that it? He knew I loved Barm's writing, and then Barm's work was banned. He knew I was inspired by Barm himself (and it is not always true that both an author and his work are admirable) and then Barm disappeared to the Island. I had never believed that Wils was directly responsible for what had happened to Barm, although I had always worried that my interest in his work, my defense of him whenever we talked about the current situation at the office were partly responsible for his arrest. I had always believed that Police or Justice were after him.

Suddenly I absolutely hated Wils. "Jump in, Wilsy," I said, holding the boat steady. Wils gave my arm a quick squeeze as he climbed in. He had been looking at me very fondly those past days, and anyone with eyes—and Serena had nothing if she did not have eyes—must have seen that something was going on. Even I had seen it with Wils and Anny on the Mountain, and that was mild compared with how Wils and I had been.

I pushed the boat off and jumped in and sat next to Wils in the stern. I felt Wils's thigh next to mine. I could tell he was wanting to touch me. I had intoxicated him, won him, unintentionally, but I had enjoyed my effect. He was totally wrapped up in me, and I, in spite of my saying that I did not worry about what happened next, was worried about what would happen with Wils back in the Complex. I did not fear for my own safety, despite the reports that Serena must have been accumulating, and despite whatever else might have been brewing that I did not know about. My affair with Wils had made me stronger and confident and lighthearted and happy, while Wils had been getting more and more lovesick and incapacitated. I could tell he was in agony beside me because he could not grab me right there and set a new first for us: lovemaking in a rowboat in front of a soldier, a Secret Service spy, and two Deputy Ministers of Information. The thought would have made me laugh and press my thigh against Wils to make his agony worse, if it had not been for my new awareness of how dangerous he was. I wondered how I would behave with him that night, our last night on the Peninsula. I did not know what I would do when we got back to the Complex. I had a feeling that Wils would insist on marrying me, and I had to think of a way to avoid that. I had cared for him in a way. Yet I knew I had to refuse him gently and keep myself alive and active and out of detention all at the same time so that I could free Lak and Barm and everyone else. But Wils could have me sent off at any time.

The deputies took a while to get used to rowing. The water was a little choppy, and we slapped up and down and lurched to the right and left as they got used to pulling their oars in the same direction at the same time. Wils was laughing, and the deputies were laughing. The soldier just stared off, as if he were waiting for a bus, and Serena made a show of wincing whenever one of the deputies whisked water onto her skirt with his oar. I tried to laugh along with the others. There was a current that helped us on our way, and despite the puny abilities of the deputies, we were out beyond the lighthouse and on the open water of the straits in no time. It is hard to believe that during the revolution refugees cast themselves into these waters, in pudding basins practically, and some even survived.

Then I knew we were in trouble. The amount of water in the bottom of the boat had increased. I knew it was not just from the amount slopped in by the oars.

"We should be getting back for lunch. Turn around," I said. I tried to sound normal, because I knew that if we panicked, we were lost. I am a terrible swimmer, and the others were worse.

"You keep your oar in the water," I said to one deputy, and to the other I said, "and you keep rowing this way," directing the turnaround. I was an idiot to have allowed this situation to develop. I had been intent on having a good time and caution had been thrown to the winds, as they say.

We turned about. The rowers, the soldier, and Serena now faced the straits. Only Wils and I could see how tiny the beach and villa were. There was very little chance that anyone at the villa could see us, even if they did happen to be looking out across the straits.

"Row," I said. "I've got to get back to finish the speech."

Wils looked at me. He knew we were in trouble. But he did not yet look frightened.

"I knew we had work to do," Serena said. She had folded her arms when she got in the boat and had not unfolded them.

"Serena, you are as ever so right," I said. "When we get back, you shall have a commendation. Wils will see to it."

But Wils was by this time tense and he was looking at the shore and at the water in the boat. The rowers seemed to be making no headway. Did we all just sit there in a boat that was filling with water and, as in a comedy, sink gracefully out of sight, Serena with her arms folded and lips pursed as she went under, the deputies rowing to the end, even underwater, the soldier's rifle butt sticking up like a periscope?

"We're getting nowhere," one of the deputies said finally, and he looked around and saw how far the shore still was.

Serena looked around and started yelling. "We're sinking. It's all Neila's fault. Look what she has done to us."

The deputies tried to row vigorously in the strength of their panic, and we got a little way. But the water was all over the floor of the boat, over the black shoes of Wils and the deputies, and almost over the ankles of the soldier's boots. Wils looked at me, very frightened. "Someone should swim for help," he said.

"I'll swim for help," I said. "You all bail out." And I went over the side before the others decided they wanted to, before I lost my chance. It seemed foolish to give up the only solid thing I had, but I could not just sit there and go under. I dived off to get a good way from the boat, and my sunglasses were swept off. I saw them sink down into the straits.

I expected to drown, but I preferred to drown doing something other than just sitting. I knew my strength was limited, and I decided not to look at the shore, so that I would not die seeing what I could not reach. I turned on my back and began a backstroke, slow and measured, and I gazed at the sky, watching the clouds. They banked and changed shape rapidly, and after a few moments I lost the urge to look back at the little boat and to look at the shore. I felt quite peaceful and had no desire then to look anywhere but up at the sky. I wondered who the people back at the Complex would tell. Would Lak ever find out that I had drowned? They would find my journals. I would be exposed. And even poor Wils, whose only stupidity as far as the Complex was concerned was to have an affair with me, a resister, would not die a hero. I kept going, on my back, for a long time. I did not fight the choppiness or the current. I let it all carry me, although I was able to keep myself pointed toward the shore and gauge my position by the sun. I did not think of the boat. I could not bear to think of those five going under. I would have saved them if I could. Even Wils, and even Serena. I felt I could outwit her, somehow, and I also had learned that she was not as smart as I had always believed. I had lost my fear of her.

Suddenly my heel cracked the sand, very painfully. I put my feet down and found I was in water that was knee-deep. In fact, I had been swimming needlessly for the past hundred meters, when I could have been walking. The floor of the straits sloped gradually up to the beach, and while I still had another fifty meters to go, I was able to stand up and run, a nightmare kind of run, through water that pulled against my legs and held me back. I took a quick look out to the middle of the straits, but the wind had strengthened and the water was choppier, and I could see nothing. I ran screaming up the beach, screaming to the soldiers to help, help, help, and I fell down, my cheek on the warm sand.

I recall hardly anything of the trip back to the Complex. But I became aware, after a few days, that I was in a hospital. They told me that the soldiers on shore had got motorboats and searched for the rowboat but had found nothing. Then air force planes has searched. I am ill at the recollection, nauseated, wretched. Truly I had expected to drown, too.

I hit my foot in such a way on the sand that I bruised a bone, and I limp as I walk. I am exhausted at my life. I deserve to die, too. I seem to damage everyone I touch.

The five who drowned were given a major memorial service. I was expected to give an address, and I was able to pull myself together enough to give the Peninsula speech that I had written for Wils. I still wanted my message to get out, and I told the mourners that Wils would have wanted it. That is not really a lie. He would have given that speech, because of his regard for me, if for no other reason.

Every day I go through the lists of political prisoners on the

Island, but I still cannot find Lak's name. Either I have missed it or the list is incomplete. Both are possible. Or else he is not there at all.

A discussion today during coffee in the lounge stays with me. It was strange to be there without Wils. The discussion went like this: if a man attempts to pick a pocket, and the pocket is empty, and the man is caught, is he guilty? Has a crime been committed? If a woman wishes to kill a man and puts an aspirin in his tea, believing erroneously that aspirin is fatal, and the man drinks the tea and nothing happens, is she guilty of attempted murder? If a tribal man wishes an enemy dead and the man lies down and dies, is it murder?

Because I left Wils and Serena and the deputies and the soldier in that boat and swam to the shore to get help, and to save myself, too, and at the same time had wanted them out of the way many times, am I a murderer?

The last possibility, of course, was not discussed. It is my own question to myself. I was sitting with two lawyers, eminent young men with great futures, both of whom specialize in such questions. One is writing a book on attempted crime, and the research has so pleased the Complex that he has been given a house in the country and a year on full pay to write on the issue. I began by taking a lively interest in the discussion. I am always interested in versions of the truth. Then, as always happens now, I began to think of the drownings and my role, and I got quieter and more withdrawn. Being lawyers, they did not notice. They leaned forward, talking directly to each other, their heads coming together in front of me.

Afterwards I walked home rather than wait for the office car. They don't like me doing this. We have some kind of policy of keeping people of importance out of sight as much as possible, for protection they say, but of course it also enables them to keep an eye on us. However, they seem to let me do what I want for the moment, given what I have been through and given that I am Acting Minister. But when I walk I usually discover that the car is following me some distance behind.

I stopped off to buy toothpaste and hand lotion at the chemist, which is next to the hospital I was in after the Peninsula accident. To cater to the patients and visitors to the hospital the chemist also sells cosmetics, writing pads, socks, combs, and the like. The socks on display are white, black, or gray cotton. The woolen ones are kept behind the counter in a glass case, which is kept locked. No one ever buys them because they cost too much, but the Complex believes that the presence of such goods helps morale and image. The woolen socks can be pointed at to show that things are not as bad as rumor has it.

I prowled around the store a little, choosing my toothpaste and just filling in time. I don't know why I should be so aimless since I have a great deal ahead of me to accomplish. A man, tall, thin, skinny really, was looking through the cotton socks. I stood and watched him and as I watched he swept half a dozen pairs off the rack and into a brown paper bag he was holding. Then he looked up and saw me watching him. I stared back at him and said nothing. He waited for me to call out, to do something. I walked up to the counter and paid for my toothpaste, fumbling for the exact change. The man, I sensed, was walking out the door, with the bag of socks.

"That man just stole some socks," I said to the sales clerk.

"What man?"

"He just walked out," and I nodded toward the door.

I left quickly and jumped into my car, which had pulled up outside. I told the driver to get me home quickly and we sped off, while the sales clerk was running up and down the street, looking for the man. I told the driver to hurry, for suddenly I felt that I could get killed. In examining that feeling now I think I must have been frightened by the thief's eyes. He did not look guilty or innocent. He was bold, staring at me, daring me to make a fuss. I felt that he would have liked to kill me. But he got away with the socks and I am unharmed. I let him go. It was not because I believe that such thefts are a blow against the

Complex and I was on his side. I think you have to pay for what you take. I was frightened, and a coward. He had had a good chance to look at my face and commit it to memory.

I have found an old tub to take the press to the Island. An old ferry. If the weather is bad, it could take two days instead of fifteen hours. I am furious. Wils could have procured one of the newest boats. Poor Wils. I am lucky he is dead. But I have no real power. They are all just putting up with me until they can organize a new minister. They are using me — and I am also using them.

The tub lists somewhat, but I have decided we will go. I can't hesitate now and waste more time trying to get a better boat, although I do wish I had not committed myself to any action or change. I have just had a meeting with the cabinet in which I explained that it was intelligent and original to take the press to the Island. It seems that none of the ministers has even been there and no one knows what it is really like.

Somehow word has got out that we are going, and at the dock this morning, when I went down to take a look at the boat, there were dozens of people, women mainly, waiting, sitting there, with baskets of things — food, clothes, books — hoping to press them upon me and the others as we boarded, planning to implore us to locate a missing son or friend. Their mission was like mine. I hesitated for a moment, then I told the assistant to take the baskets and packages quickly and assure the people that we would do our best. I told him to tell them to disappear, not to embarrass the Acting Minister and her guests from overseas.

They labeled their baskets, handed them in, and disappeared. But when we came back to the dock to board and set sail, there were dozens more waiting with baskets and packages. Friends of friends of friends. This time I was really worried for my safety. The photographers were there, foreign, not domestic, snapping the assistant gathering the baskets, interviewing some of the women who had waited all day and had stories of having had a member of their family hauled off, presumably to the Island. But because we were on the point of setting sail, the reporters could not send off any stories, so the photographs and reports had to travel with them on the journey, and I was given a re-prieve of a few days before the world would know.

For the first time it has occurred to me that I could be sailing into my own exile. What if the Complex has realized what I am up to and just plans to leave me on the Island? But of course I am somewhat protected by all these cameras and reporters.

This is possibly the worst place on earth, because the prisoners live so primitively and even more because the rain falls for three hundred days a year. There is always water on the ground. There is nowhere to feel dry and warm. The sun came out for a mo-ment today, and in a mud puddle on the road I saw the blue sky and clouds reflected, a little puddle of beauty. But if I were to kneel down to look closely, if I hoped to catch it and understand it and recall it later after the rain had begun again, I would see only muddy water, and in kneeling to look in this little mirror I would get my knees muddy and my hands would sink into the slush and I would achieve nothing. I would be damper and colder and worse off than before.

I am appalled, sick at the whole thing. I had no idea it was like this. The Complex has sent ten thousand people here. There was no one here before. It was an uninhabited island. And for good reason. The first load of prisoners came in a boat, one thousand or so, I believe. It was a ferry similar to the one we have been given for this visit. The ferry moored just off the island and the prisoners had to jump out, with nothing. They had to wade and swim ashore to an island where it rains three hundred days a year, where there was nothing. No shelter, no food.

One thousand men and women were turned out one day and had to survive. And every now and then more boatloads arrived and dumped new prisoners, like rubbish dumped overboard. Each new boatload with the need for food and shelter threatened to destroy the tenuous little system that the previous groups had set up. The prisoners have had to give all their energy to staying alive, organizing a society. If I were them, I would have started to build some kind of boat, I think, although without tools of any sort and with no native inhabitants it would take time to get trees cut and bound together. But my guess is that there must be a raft or something in the process of being built. I imagine it could also be possible to hold onto a log and swim off, perhaps. I would also send a constant stream of messages in bottles, hoping that compassionate outsiders would come to the rescue. But I am forgetting that there are no bottles, no paper to write on. Perhaps they could scratch messages on bark and cast them off.

The southern coast of the Island is a cliff with no beach or inlet, and the ocean is rough. Any escape that way, especially on a primitive raft or boat, is unlikely. The north coast has a few beaches and since the sea floor drops quickly it is possible for a big boat to get in fairly close before it discharges its human load. We have been told that the boats depositing new prisoners sometimes send a swimmer with a long rope to the shore first and that the others are then allowed to hold onto the rope as they make their way to the land. That is the only help they get. But we have also been told that the rope is then reeled back to the boat, depriving the prisoners of even that piece of simple equipment. Imagine struggling ashore, wet, cold, to start life again from the very beginning.

The Island itself is rugged and hilly, a lot of steep hills rising almost straight from the shoreline, cut by deep little valleys which are awash with the constant rainfall. To get out of the water the prisoners have been compelled to climb to the tops of the hills, up almost sheer cliffs, and make huts or lean-tos as best they can. It seems that they have an economic and social development plan of sorts, because each new wave of prisoners is registered and directed to a new hill to settle, and what could be called villages, of up to one hundred people, have been formed. The prisoners have made some kind of lookout, which is manned twenty-four hours a day, to watch for the arrival of a ship. And some of the prisoners, who have been appointed registrars, record the names of the new arrivals, as they crawl wet and shivering from the sea onto the beach. The registrars explain the situation and indicate the next hill that is to be settled. There has been a lot of fighting among the prisoners, mainly between the new arrivals, who see that the older inhabitants have more comforts, such as huts with leaves spliced together for roofs, paths and steps cut out of the hillside, and clearings in their villages, and the established inhabitants, who are willing to provide temporary billets for the newcomers and advise and give technical assistance to them in building their own villages, but who must defend the integrity of the villages they have built up over several years with such terrible labor.

Many prisoners have died because of illness and loss of hope. There is a cemetery, well tended, with simple headstones and wild flowers all around.

The boats that bring in the prisoners quickly cast off again, usually turning around in an hour or so. They fear that the cunning prisoners may have found a way to capture them. It has been a cheap undertaking for the Complex. No prisons to be built, no wardens, no expensive equipment, no administration.

I now see that there is no way for Lak to send me a letter from here. He must have written it either before he was sent here or he is not here at all, even though I can see that these are the hills that get the sea breeze, and that you have to go everywhere on foot, just as he described in that hidden way in his first letter.

When our boat drew near the Island, we could see the exiles on the thin strip of beach, thinking, I now realize, that we were a new load being dumped. I had expected much more of a stir. When they realized that we were not another group of prisoners, there was mild excitement. I heard some little children saying to each other, "They've come to take us back home." But they were not jumping and shouting.

People started pouring into the clearing from all around, down the little paths that led from the hilltops. The registrars who sat in the middle of the clearing looked uncertain and were, of course, also angry at us. The photographers among the visiting press party were busy snapping pictures, and the reporters were talking to whoever they could. It crossed my mind that the prisoners could rise up and kill us all and take the boat. But the atmosphere remained calm. The prisoners had astoundingly good manners.

"Look, don't let anything happen to us or there'll be trouble," I said to one of the registrars somewhat unnecessarily, and then I added, "Mass executions, I assure you. The Complex will not hesitate to send out planes and ignite this little island." I had made that up, on the spur of the moment, and I surprised myself. It sounded as if it were my own idea and I really was a Complex loyalist to even think of such a thing. "It is in your interests to keep us safe. Tell us everything you want to tell us and show us everything you want to show us. These reporters are from abroad. They will take your story back home with them. The world will learn of your plight. It is your only hope, I think."

The people had filled up the clearing and were sitting cross-legged on the ground, the children, too, quiet and well-behaved, waiting for us to do something. Then I saw Mother, Lak's mother, the mother from my Complex family, making her way through the sitting people, a broad, unwavering smile on her face. Too broad a smile for a prisoner. She had grown horribly skinny. She used to be fat, really fat, and I had thought at one point that she must have had diabetes. Now she looked deathly thin, and that smile was actually terrible to see. She kept her eyes on my face, picking her way through the people, never looking down, doing it by some animal sense, not treading on anyone, smiling and not blinking. Straight at me. She came right up to me, put her arms around me, and kissed the air at the side of my cheek. Then she stood back from me and looked at me then leaned forward and kissed the air at the side of the other cheek. She had never kissed me before. In her own home in the Complex she had always been undemonstrative and somewhat circumspect, suspicious, and she had often questioned me about where I was going, with whom, administering all those tests of loyalty. (At least, that is what I thought they were at the time, tests of loyalty, and they really weren't. All the family had been wanting to know was whether I was a resister like them and could be trusted. A traditional family misunderstanding.)

Mother kept her arms around me too tightly. Her skinny body pressed against me. I leaned back from her and still she did not let go, as anyone naturally would. I felt afraid and I had to take her arms from around me, and, keeping her hands held in mine, I maneuvered her away from me and kept her at arm's length, because I could feel that if I let go she would come right back to me and pin me down with those arms of hers. This was my mother, my adopted mother, who had been carried away in the worst circumstances, whom I had worried about constantly, toward whom I felt a terrible guilt for unwittingly contributing to the family misfortune, and here I was seeing her, alive, apparently delighted to see me, even in these terrible surroundings, and I was pushing her away.

Then, when I looked up, I saw the sisters, but they were on the outskirts of the sitting crowd, and they were making no attempt to come close to me. They stood there silently and looked at me, and no smiles, no acknowledgment came from them, just anger and hatred, exactly what I would have expected, and what I deserved. They were watching the spectacle of their mother trying to embrace this treacherous adopted daughter and me trying to disentangle myself. One of the sisters came toward us through the squatting throng, carefully, quickly. She was coming to get her mother. She came right up to us, looking at me with all that hatred. She put her arm around her mother and with difficulty led her away. Mother still wanted to embrace me and stay near me.

"Sister," I said to her.

She turned and gave me another one of those looks and kept walking away. Then I realized that the cameramen had been photographing all this. The thin old woman embracing the Acting Minister of Information.

Then the Island officials, the ones I thought of as the immigration registrars, called for attention. Not that they needed to. This crowd had been sitting there quietly for fifteen minutes with no sound at all, just a bit of whispering. The effect was ghostly. I would have expected a riot, a lot of noise, a furious attack, stones, sticks, the hijack of the boat, or at least shouted epithets against these representatives of the Complex. But there was nothing. This particular Complex strategy of exile had been horribly successful. And its perpetrators back in the Complex had no idea how effective they had been.

The official held up his hands and stated that the Acting Minister wished to speak. I had been standing there the whole time, so to mark the beginning of the proceedings I stepped forward. Then I noticed that Mother had made her way back to me and was coming right up to my side again. I thought she would grab hold of me in her bony fingers and drag me away with her. She came and stood beside me. No one stopped her. The sisters did not come forward again. The photographers were photographing, still. I had to start to talk, with this specter of a person, this mother of mine, standing on my right. I was clasping my hands at my waist, a nervous way I have of doing something with my hands, and Mother, watching my every movement, clasped her hands at her waist. I stepped forward a step, and Mother stepped forward a step.

"You are heroes," I said, rather quietly and spread my hands, palms up, toward the crowd. Mother spread her hands toward them, too. People could not hear me well, because those farthest away leaned their heads toward each other, as if asking "What did she say? What did she say?" At least that leaning movement of their heads showed me they were alive, human.

"You are heroes," I said, shouting really, "and soon all this will be over." Then I was aware that Mother was muttering my exact words.

"Heroes," I heard her say, and "will be over."

"I am overwhelmed at the agony I see here. I had no idea," I said.

"Here. No idea," Mother echoed, moving her hands exactly as I moved mine.

Then I knew that she was mad. Back in the Complex, at her own house, when we were all there together (at a time that now seems so long ago and so peaceful even though I was always hurting from the death of my real parents), whenever a mad person passed by or came begging for food the people in the street would laugh and point and the children would tease. Mother, though, would send one of us out with food and a little money and an invitation to sleep on the veranda under a blanket. She taught her children charity. The peculiar sight of a mad woman standing beside an official and mimicking her seemed to cause no reaction in this crowd, not even a smile. I turned to Mother and found myself putting my arm around her and holding her to me. "Oh Mother, I am so sorry, my Mother," I said to her, softly, and she snuggled into my arm, against me, like a little child.

I wished I had never embarked on this journey. I wished I had died long ago and had been spared all this. I thought I would die soon anyway, and at that moment I felt I had nothing more to lose. I did not care if the Complex arrested me, killed me, or even if the political prisoners rose up and tore me apart. One way or another I deserved it, and wanted it. I kept my arm tightly around my mother.

"Courage, all of you," I said. "We shall see to it that this terrible mistake is rectified. And we shall have you all home in no time." I had no idea how I was going to do that.

"No time," Mother said.

I spoke on a bit. Then I saw someone in the crowd moving.

He was getting to his feet, and I saw who it was. It was Barm. I went forward to him.

"Barm," I said when I was close.

He gave me that look of hatred, like the sisters. He was emaciated and looked like an old man. Mother trailed along at my side. "Barm, Barm, Barm," she muttered, and giggled. Giggled.

Barm was trying to leave the gathering. That had been his intention in standing up. When I called his name he spat on the ground.

"Barm, wait, don't leave." When I was close to him I said, "I'm taking you back with me. You can't stay on here. You will be free. I can do that for you."

He laughed at me. And he threw his arms out wide, indicating the hundreds of prisoners sitting there on the ground.

"See these people?" he said. "And there are thousands more up in those hills, struggling to stay alive. I'm not leaving this Island until every one of them is free. I'm going to be the last to leave."

"Barm, I had no idea there was anything like this Island. I'm going to try to get everyone released. But in the meantime," and I had raised my voice again so that more people could hear, "I am going to take three hundred of you with me. I think that is how many the ferry will take. It won't be a pleasant journey, but it won't be long, and you will be set free when we get to the Complex harbor. And then we will have to find a way to get the rest of you off."

"You do that," Barm called out. "And I'm still going to be the last one to leave." But he stayed on, listening, instead of leaving the group. He stayed and listened to what I had to say.

"I want three hundred people," I repeated. "You decide who it should be. But since you will have to wade ashore secretly at the Complex," (I was making up these plans as I was talking, ad-libbing frantically, hoping that I came up with something practical) "it would be better to choose those who are strong and can take care of themselves for a while once they are back."

I was expecting a kind of stampede to the boat, when I said that, but again there was scarcely any reaction.

"We need the strong ones here," Barm shouted. "We don't stay alive here by basking in the sun, you know."

I turned to the registrars. "You choose three hundred. We have to leave in an hour."

One official announced to the crowd, "Three hundred of you must go. Who wants to? I would say ten from each village. Come forward and wait on the beach."

A few people straggled forward and a few of the very young men seemed eager to go. I could not believe it. I was forcing this rescue on these miserable wretches and risking everything. The officials went through the crowd touching on the shoulder those they decided should come with us.

I went and spoke with Barm, Mother beside me, of course.

"Barm, please, come back with us."

He sneered at me. "I am not leaving my people."

"But they don't even want to come," I said. I was practically crying. "They won't let me rescue them."

"Why should they?" Barm said. "Why should they give you that glory?"

"Barm, what if I left you with paper and pens. Will you write everything down that has happened? Will you?"

He laughed at me. "Look at this," he said, sweeping his arms around again, "and you talk of paper and pens."

"Someone has to write it down," I said.

"Then you write it down," he replied. "You go home and sit down and write it all down. As for me, I've grown beyond paper and pens. Shall I tell you how? I am working every day to stay alive. And I write in my head as I work. I am writing a novel, and it is written in my head. Every day I start off by reciting it from the beginning, and when I get to the end of what I have composed so far, I add the next paragraph and memorize that. I have a novel in my head. It is nearly finished. I can recite it, but I will never put it down on paper. A waste of time. If you want it, you'll have to take my head."

I wondered if he, too, was mad. And yet I felt chastened, ashamed of every aspect of myself. The officials had rounded up several hundred prisoners and were ordering them into lines, ready for the plunge back into the water and the wading to the boat. I had had the ferry brought in as close as possible and ropes brought ashore to help guide the people to it. I felt I was taking them into exile, to their deaths, rather than saving them. Barm was walking away by then. He had started reciting his novel at me, like a taunt, and it began, "My story is in my head and if you want it you'll have to take my head to get it."

I felt I was going mad. After Barm's taunts I had the urge to tell him that I was staying, that I would be the last to leave the Island. He made me want to compete with him, and I realized I was also angry with him for making everything so much harder for me. "Then write your novel and keep it in your head," I wanted to yell after him. Then I was ashamed of my pettiness as I confronted on that Island the worst human disaster that I could possible imagine. The only worse thing would be the slaughter of these people, but then I was not sure if death would really be worse than this.

Barm kept on reciting as he went, and I felt so angry that I went right through the crowd toward the sisters. They thought I was coming to deliver their mother back to them. They still said nothing to me.

"Sisters," I said quickly, "I had no idea about all this. I had no idea you were resisters, too."

"'What do you mean, 'too'?" said one.

"I mean that I am a resister, and I always was, and I thought you were loyal Complexers, and now I see that you thought I was, and that is why we could never talk much about anything that mattered. That's why we were always guarded with each other."

"Except Lak, who you won over all right," said the sister.

"Except Lak," I said. "Where is he? Is he safe? He didn't

know, either, about me being a resister.''

The sister gave me a long look. "You don't know where he is? You're Acting Minister of Information and you don't know?"

"How come you're a Complex dignitary, then, if you're a resister?" asked a second sister.

"We have people inside and outside. You know that," I said. "You should know it. You were inside."

"Until you set us up for arrest," she said.

"I did not set you up. Look, I'm taking three hundred people back with me. And look at what the press is going to write. I'm going to be dead very soon."

"It's too late to take them out. The damage has been done to us all."

And I knew what she meant. "But what about Lak? I really don't know anything." I was begging. "Please let me know, is he dead, too?"

All the dead men of my life, all the men I have cared for. Mother was clinging to me again, but I was again able to reverse my natural impulse to step away from her. I put my arm around her, turning her into the receiver and me into the strong one, and I gave her the protection she was wanting. That gesture of mine seemed to make the sisters talk a bit. They clearly were still not sure of me. "Is he dead?" I asked again, and Mother started to cry.

"No, no, Mother," said one of the sisters. "Lak is not dead. Lak is alive. Of course he is. He wouldn't die. Not our Lak." Then she looked at me. "Lak escaped before we were arrested, the day you left on your trip."

And that second sister, the suspicious one, interrupted. "She knows all this. She knows why she left on that trip and what happened to us all."

"I swear I don't." Several people had gathered around and were listening. I wanted them to hear me. "I know nothing of all this," I said to them.

"The day you left on your trip with those friends of yours—" the first sister went on.

"Do you know what happened to them? Do you have any idea?" I said, half crying. "Wils is dead, drowned, and so is Serena. Leo and Anny I know nothing about. Probably dead, too, somewhere. I haven't heard a thing. I saw Wils and Serena drown. And now I am working to free all of you and no one seems to want it. Look." I pointed to the prisoners lining up for the escape, who were acting as if they were about to be exterminated.

"How can they trust you?" said the suspicious sister. "How do they know they aren't going to be dumped out in the middle of the ocean to drown? Why didn't you just drown us all? Why even this piece of rotten land for us?"

"The day you left," the first sister continued, "that night, they came to get us. There had been a blackout in our area, which was inconvenient. But we just shrugged it off and got out the candles. It was Lak who thought it was strange. He went off to investigate. We learned later that the Complex had deliberately turned off the electricity and disrupted communications, so that the arrests could be made more easily. No lights, no telephones, no telex abroad, just confusion. While Lak was gone they came and got the rest of us, at one a.m. At least he is alive, and will come to help us. Father is dead. He died soon after we got here. The wet, the cold, and the lack of food and shelter have killed hundreds. And look at Mother."

The crowd, although impassive, appeared to be listening. I felt this little woman against my body, this little mad woman. I should not have been so lucky. I should have been here, too. It was sheer chance that I had escaped. I was certainly stupid and naive enough to have been captured and arrested. Instead, it turned out that I was stupid and naive enough to be able to remain free. And Father, that good man with his mosquito and Beethoven theories, was dead. And Wils, who was not so good, and Serena, who was evil. And my own father and mother, who they all insist were of no political importance.

"What about Lak? I received three letters from him, some time ago. But I have no idea where he is."

"And we don't know either. One thing you can be sure of, though — it will take a lot to kill him."

A man in the crowd muttered something, fairly loudly, but I did not catch it. It was meant for me. I turned to him. "I did not hear you," I said, ready for anything. I felt so guilty I was furious. I was furious at this pathetic crowd. And then I felt more guilty for being furious. I hated seeing them all.

"I did not hear you, brother," I repeated.

"I said, that is not your mother," he said.

"You mean this woman?" I said, indicating Mother. I was still holding her against me. "She was a mother to me, and the father who died here was a father to me."

"She is not your mother. You're an impostor. I knew your mother and father. I worked with them. I saw them marry, and I saw them the day they died."

I had not expected to get this information, which I had been wanting so badly and had tried to get for so long.

"Please, tell me about them," I said.

The prisoners were being prodded into the water and, holding onto the rope, they were wading out to the boat in single file. They were silent, not really resisting after their first protests, and those they were leaving behind, perhaps a wife or child or new friend found on the Island, were wailing quietly or just watching. It all looked terrible, those blank faces and skinny bodies, filing into the water.

"Quick, tell me about my mother and father," I said to the old man who had spoken. "How did they die? What were they like?"

The man spoke at me, not really seeing me. "She was a beautiful woman. No one knew why she married your father, except that he was a good man."

"Did they resist? Were they good resisters?" I asked "Did

they love me?''

"I saw you as a baby and as a girl. They loved you enough, I should think. They resisted enough. That's not the point.''

"How did they die?''

"It was an accident. But they had been arguing that day. Then we had a group meeting and they did not talk to each other at all. And afterwards they crashed. He was driving.''

"Did the Complex do it to them?'' I thought I might faint, just pass out before I heard everything. No one had told me so much.

"The Complex? No, the Complex isn't clever enough, or wasn't then. She had been having affairs. It was generally known.''

"Who with?'' I asked.

He shrugged. "This one had been going on for months. Everyone knew. A Complex official. She sometimes laughed and said, 'All in the line of duty,' but your father did not know. We all knew. He found out that day. The official was there, at the meeting. It was clear what had been going on. There's no mistaking that kind of thing.''

"How could he do that, and leave me behind? Why didn't he come and get me, too?'' I desperately wanted to have died with them, to have been sitting there in that car, between them perhaps, as they smashed into that tree.

"He found out at that meeting, or just before it,'' the man went on.

I had tears running down my cheeks. I thanked the man. I kissed his hands. The photographers were still photographing us, snapping here and there. I didn't care. If what he said was true about the deaths of my mother and father, then I had no reason, no personal reason, to be a resister at all. I had always believed that in joining a group and resisting I was avenging their deaths.

The boat was nearly ready. The prisoners had been herded in. We had to leave.

"We'll be back," I said to the registrars. "You'll be off here soon, I promise."

On the boat the reporters were blocking out their stories ready to rush to their typewriters and get them off as soon as they landed back in the Complex. They would have to take them to the airport themselves or get someone they could trust to take them out of the Complex. The stories would never make it through the usual telex or telephone.

I did not know what I planned to do. I thought that somehow I would just have the boat go back and forth to the Island, collecting and discharging prisoners until the Complex caught on and stopped it and killed me.

But I still had to find Lak.

We had left the Island at dusk so that we would reach the Complex again at dawn, and if there was any problem with rough seas we would have the whole day to get the prisoners off and the ferry docked. That is standard practice, to travel so that you arrive early morning and give yourself the daylight to help you if you need it.

It was not light when we passed the first Complex fishing boats and saw the Complex shore. The sea was flat in this spot. It was warm and shallow and there was a certain channel the boat had to follow to get to the dock. We slowed down and stopped quite a way from the shore and again we were confronted with the problem of prisoners who did not want to escape. They did not want to get back into the water and wade to shore. That is what that terrible confinement had done to them all. They still believed that they were going to be discharged into the deep and drowned, exterminated. And they sat solidly and quietly, not moving. I had singled out one or two who seemed to be leaders, a ridiculous word for this demoralized group. At last I persuaded them that the land was close by. They could wade ashore and reassemble somewhere to continue their resistance, or they could disperse and find their homes and families.

"We don't have homes and families anymore," one of the prisoners said.

I did not care at this point what they did. I just wanted them to be free. And I did not know what I had done for them or what I wanted to do myself. That pathetic group huddled there, refusing to slip out of the boat at dawn and wade to freedom, began to seem like a nightmare.

"There's the shore," I said, pointing. I had taken two of them on deck with me. "Look, it will take you half an hour at the most to get there. We'll take you in as close as we dare. I can't have the whole Complex seeing what I'm doing. I don't want to die today. I need some more time. I need a few more days. Don't you see what I've done for you?"

Eventually they got off. It seemed to take hours. The sun was well up by the time the last one had been sent off. They were relatively inconspicuous, I thought. Since the deck was not so far from the water, they could just sit down with their legs dangling over the side practically touching the water, and they could slide off. Then the water was dotted with little heads and shoulders making for the shore. There was no wild scamble. Just this passive walking through water toward the shore.

I kept the two leaders with me. I told them that they should hijack the ferry and its crew and go back to the Island for others and keep going back and forth, even hijacking more boats. I suggested a couple of other ports they might make for, and I only hope they did what I told them. We pulled in at the dock and I got off, along with the rest of the press. We had only been gone two nights and a day.

PART IV: VALLEY

When I walked into my office building, three guards from the top floor (I noticed their armbands immediately) stepped forward. They verified my name, although they knew who I was. I showed them my card. One took me by the arm and they led me into the special elevator that went straight up to the top rather than to the 25-38 bank that usually took me to my office. They said nothing, I said nothing. But I felt fairly calm. I had been expecting the calm to come to an end, but not so soon, not the first day after the Island visit. The overseas press reports would hardly have been sent, let alone printed and received back in the Complex. The guards and I looked up and watched the floor numbers light up as we sped to thirty-nine. We stepped out onto the green carpet and went through the usual identification procedures, showing our cards, and then we were frisked, the guards included. A normal day on the thirty-ninth floor.

I was even wondering if they were bringing me there to promote me again. They could be mad and stupid enough. I had been thinking about this a lot. The resistance could succeed through sheer luck, by accident. I could become the next leader of the Complex, overnight, practically without lifting a finger, in spite of the Island visit and the press clips. And certainly without heroics. I am not indomitable. I am not a hero. I am not an activist and I do not care for groups and ostentatious political stands. I am also a coward and fearful, although I do appreciate the efforts of the brave. But as leader I could nevertheless turn everything around. I could set all the political prisoners free immediately, of course, and certainly see to it that they were received as heroes and given money to settle into a regular life again. And a memorial. I could have a memorial built to the political prisoners, who would be called POLIPRIS or POPRIS. A vale with flowers and leaves of different greens and the names of the POLIPRIS worked into the stone. VALHERA, The Vale of the Heroes, Resisters, and Activists. VALPORESI, Vale of the Political Resisters. Or just plain VAPOR. There would be a lifting of the fear and the suspicion and the terror for all. And for me personally, peace and an open search for Lak.

The guard kept on gripping my arm as we walked across the anteroom, which, although behavior is always upside down in the Complex, made me dismiss my promotion fantasy, and I felt ashamed of the delusions of grandeur that had overtaken me. Me, the coward.

A secretary who was leaning over her desk searching through some papers looked up at me as I passed. I looked back at her and she bit her lip in a worried little way and went back to her riffling. In we went to one of the inner chambers. A dozen or so people were gathered together around someone sitting down. I instantly recognized the Leader, whom I had never met, standing to one side. He keeps well out of the way, although we see his picture at every turn. The group looked at me. The guards led me up to the Leader and relinquished their grip. They handed me over. The Leader himself then took me. He actually held my arm, but much more tightly than the guards. I was mouthing politenesses and honorifics at him, as was appropriate. And I was awed. The Leader. The man who had ruined thousands, killed thousands. He led me round to face the person in the chair.

It was Serena.

"Serena!" So they had survived. I went to step forward to her, to take her hand, embrace her even, welcome her back to the living. But the Leader kept his hold on me and I had to

142

stand beside him looking at her. She was thin and sunburned and gave me a look, I don't know how to describe it, of hate, excitement.

"Serena, you are safe. Where are the others? What happened?" And I started to cry. I meant it. It was a terrible shock to see her there.

"You see how upset she is to see me alive," Serena said. "She is crying. All her plans are ruined now."

This is the end of me, I thought. The very end. Although I did not know what Serena was about to say.

"Where is Wils? And the deputies and that soldier in his boots? We searched for you for days." I was talking and crying. I wanted to put my hands over my eyes, but I still could not move the arm gripped by the Leader. I used my one free hand and pressed my knuckles into one eye and then the other. I was already realizing that I need not feel like a murderer anymore. Except that I did leave them in that boat to swim to shore. I should have stayed. That would have been more heroic, and then I could have been saved, too, like Serena. But then there would have been no Island visit, no Acting Minister, nothing accomplished except my being guilt-free.

"Shall I tell her what happened, or should I wait until the trial?" Serena asked.

"Tell her," said the Leader. "It is not yet certain there will be a trial. We have to hear everything first. We do have a judicial system."

And Serena told me. The secretary from outside had come in with her note pad and pulled up a chair, still biting her lip and frowning, as if studiously thinking about something else, as if not there at all, and she kept this up the whole time that she took verbatim notes as Serena spoke.

"This is the new chief resister," Serena started off, pointing in my direction.

I felt like looking behind me, to see who she was pointing at. "Me?" I said, squeaked. "You mean me?" I think I was flattered, even excited at the thought.

"Look at her," said Serena. "What an actress."

I was actually thrilled. Chief Resister. But of course she was wrong. I would like to be Chief Resister material, but I am not. I never will be.

"She planned the whole drowning incident," said Serena. "She intended not only to get rid of me, loyal Complex servant, but also the two Deputy Ministers of Information and the faithful soldier. Hungry to become chief of the resisters, she also planned to get rid of Wils, traitor to the Complex and himself chief of the resisters. And she did this, just as I was on the point of exposing them both. As Wils's second-in-command, she planned the whole trip to the Peninsula with this in mind. She had it all set up. The only thing Wils did not know was that he was to be included in the execution. What treachery, to be a traitor not only to the Complex, but also to her friends, that is to say our enemies, the resisters. A worm of the lowest order."

I had been standing up throughout all this. I felt like a moron trying to comprehend something too difficult. Wils? Chief Resister? Is that what she was saying? Wils? That Wils of mine? Why didn't he tell me? In all that lovemaking, why didn't he give me that crucial piece of information? Why did he let me think he was a Complexer through and through? What about all that Barm business?

I felt my lips trying to form a W, to say Wils's name. "W-w," and when I finally said "Wils," the very name made me dizzy. I could see him in that boat, I still can, sitting there frightened, and going down. Why hadn't he learned to swim?

I asked if I could sit down. They said they could not see why not.

Serena looked around. "You see what an actress, pretending to be overcome. And of course it is significant that Wils was her mother's lover."

They brought a little chair forward. It seemed tiny. I sank onto it, perched on it, rather, in the middle of that chamber on that carpet in front of Serena, skinny, brown Serena, all smiles, in her big chair with big arms, and I tried to absorb what she had just said, this latest piece of information about Wils and my mother.

"Where is Wils?" I asked. "Can I see him?"

"The others are all definitely dead," said Serena. "You will be pleased to have that confirmed. They drowned all right, as you planned. After you had set that boat up with the holes in the bottom and induced us all, forced us—she did force us, you know, ordered us—to get in and row out to sea."

"I got in, too, remember," I said.

"But you knew you could swim and we couldn't, and you came all prepared in shorts and bare feet. The rest of us were weighted down by our clothes and shoes. She had it all beautifully worked out." Serena looked radiant.

"It's not my fault that the lot of you kept on dressing as if you were about to go to a funeral," I said.

"The boat went down," said Serena. "She dived off, saying she would get help, and with the last push with her feet as she dived, she was able to make the boat go down even faster. The deputies, poor creatures, clung to the boat, and the soldier. I tried to hold the boat up. I tried to save them all. I even tried to save Wils, although the world is better off without him, so that he could be brought to trial. But the boat went down and they went under."

"And you?" I asked. "How is it you didn't go under, too, in that skirt and petticoat and those folded arms?" You rotten, lying bitch, piously mouthing loyalties. Serena, as is always apparent, saves herself first.

"When I saw there was no hope for the others, I managed to get a piece of wood, a seat from the boat or a plank from some part, and I held onto it for many days and nights in that water. I was carried out into the straits. I saw land, but I was too weak even to try to propel myself toward it. I was washed up finally, somewhere, and I walked back to the Complex. It has taken all these weeks.''

That last part I do believe. If anyone could survive hanging onto a bit of wood and walking hundreds of kilometers, Serena with her rotten tenacity and obtuseness could. I also believe she hit the others over the head with that piece of wood, held them under, did something to make sure they all drowned, so that she could come back and tell this untrue story about me. All in her good cause.

"Lolico," said Serena, and fell back in her chair. She was offered a glass of water.

"Lolico," everyone murmured in reply. Some of them swallowed and a guard actually dabbed at the corner of his eye and snuffled.

"You murderer," I found myself saying.

Serena looked around happily. "And now she comes back and takes over Information, accuses others of the crime she has committed, and no doubt she is planning a promotion for herself. Today Chief Resister, tomorrow Complex Leader."

So, Wils and my mother were lovers.

I am sitting in a room that looks out onto a flagged terrace and beyond that a garden. The room has double doors that open onto the terrace. Around the door climb roses, small ones that do not have much smell. Three long tendrils of roses have broken away from the wall and are hanging across the doorway at face level. They need to be pruned and shored up. If I cared more, if I were a little more public-spirited, I would see to it that they were taken care of. As it is, they fall across the doorway and if I don't duck when I walk out, the thorns poke me. I duck under them and step into the soft square of earth where one of the flagstones is missing and weeds are growing up. I can hear a tennis ball being hit, somewhere nearby. But I can't tell from which direction. The servants, perhaps, are having a game.

I remember a story book that my mother read to me when I was a child. It is the story of a girl who gets lost, or else she has

146

run away and is trying to get back home. She is in her night-gown. She comes to a fork in the road. One way is smooth and easy and sunny, altogether alluring. The other is dark, narrow, difficult. Thorny bushes reach out from all sides, uneven stones are underfoot. She is supposed to choose this path, but she doesn't. She chooses the easy way, which, predictably I now see, diminishes into a path worse than the one she has rejected and it takes her ever farther from home.

I like those thorns outside my door. I like ducking under them, losing my balance for a moment in the soft bit of earth, then emerging into the sunlight.

I am waiting for my trial. They are calling it a hearing, because the Leader won't say I am guilty yet. Why, I don't know. He does not need to stick up for me. Clearly I will be found guilty and I will be yet another political prisoner, unless they execute me. So I intend to walk out of here and escape. I will go to the Mountain. There is nowhere else I can think of. I would stay here if I thought I could get Serena convicted of something and put away. She must have done away with all of them in the boat. If she could grab a piece of wood and save herself, why couldn't they all have done so?

It is odd, it could be said ironic, that I am arrested for Wils's death, and not because of the Island trip.

I have been sitting here just thinking about everything—Wils, my mother and father, trying to imagine them in a group, and Lak. And I still find it impossible to imagine Wils and my mother in bed together. Serena often lies, of course, and she could be wrong about them.

It has been raining a lot. There is one drip that comes solidly from the roof, straight down onto a leaf on the vine outside my doors. Its monotony is pleasant and soothing, unlike a dripping tap or the tapping of a hammer or typewriter in the room. There was a beetle caught in my room last night. It sounded like a turbo-prop engine flashing around the room, hitting things, buffeting the light. Maddening. I had to chase it out. But outside, when I walk at night through the garden and the nearby fields, the humming of the beetles as they fly past my face is comforting.

The sound of the tennis ball, it turns out, comes from the neighboring property and I have learned that Altner is held in that house. When I walk in the grounds of my cottage, I can glimpse the road outside and I have observed crowds of people, mostly very young. Now I understand that they are there for Altner, keeping up the vigil where he is imprisoned. And I think they will give the cover I need to walk out of here.

I am treated quite well and politely. The servants still address me with respect and I have been allowed to send for some personal things. I have had *The Sacred Journey* and my journals sent over. I have wrapped them in oilcloth stolen from the kitchen and buried them in that soft square of earth, the spot with the missing flagstone. And I asked the gardener to put in a new stone so that I would not sprain my ankle every time I left my room. That was the reason I gave him.

Last night I had a dream in three parts. First, I was in a theater or a conference room. I was in the last and highest row. The place was packed. Attendance was compulsory. We were there to watch the execution of a war criminal. He was at the front, in a glass cage. Because of the distance I could hardly see him. He looked small and blurred. I could see that he was bald. They went to strap his wrists to the chair and he kept moving his arms. They had to pin him down before they could buckle the straps over his wrists. When they went to secure his body to the chair he stood up, still held to the chair by his wrists. He would not cooperate. Someone came running on with a white cloth, as if it were a net and a wild animal had to be caught. (When I was a child I used to try to use a bedsheet to catch my pets—rabbits mostly—if they got out of their pen.) They threw the cloth over the criminal, who was immediately subdued. He sat back in the chair and they strapped him down. Then they removed the cloth.

"Do we have to watch?" I asked my companion.

"Compulsory," he said.

I tried to look to one side, but I could still see the body move and the head fall forward as the gas pellets did their job. It was clear that he was a criminal and deserved to die. I could not bear to see it.

In the second part of the dream I made friends with a man I dislike in reality. He is a Complex lackey, who works in Information. In real life he is insignificant, except that I dislike him. He has a stoop, a curved back which thrusts his head and arms forward so that his hands are always in his lap or up near his face. His curved back is the result of plain bad posture, not illness or deformity. Although he and I have attended the same meetings, and in my early days in Information we were introduced, he never acknowledged me in any way until I became Acting Minister, and then he began greeting me in his squeaky little voice in the customary way. When he sits he always fidgets and jigs up and down in his chair. He can't sit still. The only lively comment I ever heard at those tedious meetings was from someone sitting behind me who said, referring to him, "It is perfectly clear that the poor man needs to masturbate in public, and someone should ask him not to."

While this man has no role in my life, I can see from what I have just written that he has had an effect on me and that he makes me very angry. In the dream he greeted me in a very friendly way and we discovered that we both spoke the language of that former student of mine, Odi, the one with the clip-on sunglasses, which in reality is not true. Neither he nor I speak that language. "I wish I had known this earlier," he said to me. "We could have been friends all this time." That language gave us a great deal in common in the dream.

In the third part I was standing in the Complex waiting for a bus. I got on one that was very crowded, asking if it passed my home. "No, we don't go near your home," the driver yelled.

"We go straight up, to Green Street." So I had to get off at the next stop, which was in a most unsafe neighborhood, and I had to run back to the first stop, to wait for the right bus. I found I was in a pair of white socks, with no shoes, and I had to run along the rough road through old tins and rubbish scattered about. My socks kept slipping down and working their way off my feet altogether. And they got dirtier and dirtier.

I am going to be found guilty of the wrong thing. I did not cause the drownings, but I did help several hundred resisters escape from the Island, which no one seems to have found out yet. I am also guilty of disliking the Complex a great deal and hoping for the overthrow of its leaders.

I can only speculate that the press reports about the Island have bought me time, since to get rid of me totally would confirm the reports. I can now see why the Leader said, "It is not yet certain there will be a trial." He wants a public trial, all according to the right procedures, so that I can be found guilty, but not because of the trip to the Island, which after all was officially sanctioned. It would make him and the whole wretched Complex look really stupid if they tried to disown that trip. He wants me to be found guilty of murder, and even to be denounced as Chief Resister (that idea still makes me smile). Once they can announce the fall of the Chief Resister they can also announce, yet again, that the resistance has been wiped out.

I intend to flee, and I suppose it won't be too hard.

I walked out of my room after dinner, avoided the thorns, trod on the new flagstone, and left that cottage. The servants must have been busy with cleaning up or, if they saw me, would have assumed that I was going for a walk. I took nothing with me, just to give the impression that I was taking a stroll. I wore the light robe I sleep in and rubber thongs, and I had taken the light cotton cover from my bed to wrap around my shoulders. They were used to my walking like that in the evening. I left all my journals and *The Sacred Journey* behind, buried beneath that new flagstone, a little square grave, and I'll have to go back one day to get them. Even if everything is burned to the ground before I ever get back, my things will be safe in the earth.

I was able to walk for a while among the hundreds of Altner fans, and then, that first night, I just kept walking. Because the house was near the edge of the Complex, I was well into the Field by dawn. I cut across the fields, keeping away from the roads, following the little paths and ridges among the crops. Where the land was flooded I walked in the water, ankle-deep, to leave no tracks, and I tried not to break down the new crops that were growing, not wanting to offend the Fielders or destroy their labor. The Fielders are good with water. They can make it stay on the sloping ground and they can keep it spread out on flat land.

It was easy going at first. The land was flat and I was used to wandering around alone in the dark. Also, I trusted the Fielders. But I was not certain what story to tell, how to account for myself when I met people, which I was sure to do. I knew I needed help from the local people, the Fielders of each village. I needed food and I was hoping to find some kind of transport, since I had hundreds of kilometers to go, and I needed clothes. My thongs had broken and I had discarded them. The bed cover became too hot to wear in the morning and I tore it in two and wrapped one half around me to try and make myself look more like a Fielder woman. The other half I tore up and wrapped around my feet. I must have looked odd, nevertheless.

The first Fielders I came across at dawn were walking to their fields. They appeared to take no notice of me as they passed. Then, when I looked around at them after they had gone by, I saw they had all stopped and were staring at me.

"Little dog," I called, "lost." Then, since that sounded pleasant, I repeated it shouting, "Lost little dog."

The Fielders looked at each other, made the crazy sign with their fingers on their foreheads, and continued on their way. I realized that I had hit upon a way to get me through difficult situations and I gradually perfected my performance. I started muttering "Lost little dog" as soon as I saw the next group walking toward me across a field on a raised, narrow path. I gestured and pointed in all directions, and even turned right around once or twice. By the time we came face to face they had deduced that I was mad and they stepped off the narrow path into the field to let me pass.

It is not my style to act like that, drawing such attention to myself, and I am still surprised that I managed to do it. In the end I even felt mad, and at times I felt I really was looking for a lost little dog. A boy outside one village asked me what the dog looked like and I told him pure black. Then his father came up and asked me what it looked like and I said black and white.

"She said pure black," the boy said, and the father hustled him away.

Because I was mad, people gave me food and drink. I would go to the back of a restaurant and sit down by the kitchen door and they would bring me out scraps. I slept outdoors while I was in the Field, where it was warm. Sometimes I got rides on empty carts returning from the market. I muttered a lot to deter people from interrupting me with questions. At times, when I saw my reflection in a window or a flooded field I got frightened. This transformation had been too easy for me.

After a while I stayed on the road, thinking that I need no longer hide in the fields. Cutting across the fields also took much longer. After many days, I had lost count of days, I came into N., the first large town I dared enter. Almost immediately I saw the same little old man we had seen on our first trip to the Mountain. He was still selling lottery tickets, no longer the special GASTRO tickets, but regular COMPLOT tickets. His white pajamas still billowed and I was afraid he would recognize me. So I squatted down and held out my right hand, as if I were a beggar, and with my left hand I shaded my eyes and hid my face to show shame, as beggars are supposed to do. This was a new performance, which surprised me as much as my crazy act.

The vendor of lottery tickets stopped right in front of me and put some money in my hand. Somehow, because my face felt hidden by my hand, I felt removed from that street. And his kind gesture, giving me a couple of coins, his touching my hand with his as he placed the coins there, made me want to cry, just silent tears. I felt hopeless. I had to walk for weeks, alone, toward a mountain. And I had no one at all. No one knew I was coming. No one cared. And I did not know what I was heading for.

"Peace, little one, and may God care for you in the days to come as you journey," the vendor said. That was not a traditional blessing to beggars. It was closer to the blessing that fathers give to daughters when they leave home or marry. It seemed as if he knew all about me and had chosen those words deliberately.

"My father, I thank you," I answered. And because my answer, calling him father, also was not traditional for a beggar, he came closer and stooped down and took my left hand away from my face. He looked into my eyes and laid his right hand on my head. I looked back at him. I felt an elation that is still hard for me to describe. I felt that from that thin hand on my head strength poured into me, and that from those old eyes I was receiving great amounts of love and courage. I lowered my eyes. At least it could be a sign that I would reach the end of my journey safely. I also thought from the way he was looking at me so intently that he was trying to place me and was remembering that I had been one of that conspicuous party of Complex tourists. Also, a young mad woman begging is not such a common sight and would seem to call for closer inspection. But his closeness to me and his touch had made me give up my pretenses. I just kept on squatting there, not muttering or twitching or doing any of the other little tricks that had become second nature during those past days.

The man told me to go and get something to eat. He gave me some more money and pointed to the little restaurant where

Serena, Anny, Leo, Wils, and I had had lunch that day. He took me straight through the restaurant to the kitchen and asked the cook, who was also the owner, to let me have a bath upstairs. He took off his own clean white shirt and gave it to me. He was wearing another shirt underneath, and I saw that he probably wore all the clothes he owned and had no fixed place to live. Perhaps he slept in the restaurant kitchen or on someone's back veranda. Although his clothes were old, they were brilliant, clean, white, and well ironed.

By this time it must have been apparent to him that I was not a mad woman. I just did what he instructed me to do. The cook gave me a kettle of warm water, which I took upstairs with me to the bathroom. I felt both helpless and, for no good reason, secure. The ticket seller's touch and the cook's showing me that little bit of care (in the Field warm water is usually given only to the elderly or the ill or someone of rank) were responsible for this. As I stood there and poured the wonderful water over me, I wondered if all this meant that I should stay in the Field and not try to get to the Mountain again, where I was not even certain of my reception by my relatives. Perhaps I could work in this restaurant, find a little place to live. Perhaps the ticket vendor needed someone to take care of him. I guessed that he laundered his own shirts and dried them quickly every day at midday and possibly borrowed some servant's iron. And even then he had time to notice someone else in need.

I washed my hair, and I washed out the bed cover half and the night robe I had been wearing, and wrung them out. I had discarded the strips of cloth around my feet long before. They had been useless. The ticket vendor's shirt felt soft and light. It came far down my thighs, almost to my knees, and I thought that I could hang out the cover and the robe in the sun behind the restaurant and that I could sit near them and comb and dry my hair while they dried, before I went in to get something to eat. When I opened the bathroom door I found that a blue cloth, a pair of blue thongs, and a comb had been placed on the floor outside the door. I did not doubt that they were meant for me. I wrapped the blue cloth around me so that it formed a long skirt and I tucked the long ends of the vendor's shirt into it. I felt wonderful. Renewed. I went downstairs and hung out the wet things and then stood under some kind of beautiful tree combing my hair. I heard birds singing and the kitchen pots clattering. I thought I might even burst into song myself.

Elar leragt niwud ildke jnas hiksad imak asagt adlak nawalb hirip hakes dupmagn remat jnedat jni rijed iwadu jni nubinamadab imak sutnugd dasjnugt. Iwanam nednow elar leragt asagt jnegtasib inepaljna jnedat nubirijjnudak nawalb iwadu nawalb jnegtasib inepalnubit jninet asagt, jnasjni jnegtasib uaw jnegtar detnem nubidasjnugd jnas ijnegtasibnubit. Nednumud nesahatetnubit jnedat jnagid nubihubek elar jnasjni hataj dasjnugt. Neg jnagid nubihubek belemuk dasjnugt jni nubisana imak najapmelib imak hubek. Hirip nubmak jirij nubijapmel nednumud elar hirasas uaw nesasepalnubit jninetnow nubihijjnab nednajnab jni agilj jnin jnagid nubihubek nednajnab ildke.

When unmarried boys and girls go out to work in the fields or in the gardens, they decorate their hair with combs. If there is an unmarried youth who wants to marry a certain girl or a girl wants a youth to marry her, he or she then takes the comb of the desired one. Then it is received by the parents of the one who owns the comb. If they recognize the comb as belonging to their child, the parents of both the girl and the youth come together for a discussion. When their discussion is over, the two young people are married, but the wedding takes place in the house of the bride's parents.

I was surprised to find myself reciting from *The Sacred Journey*. I had no youth to marry, no parents, and no house to get married in. And I became subdued again.

I took the kettle back to the cook.

"I could work here," I said. "I wouldn't be any trouble. I

can cook, or clean up. I need work.''

The man looked at me. "Go in and eat," he said. "Eat a lot. You are too thin. We can talk about work afterwards.''

He pointed into the restaurant, meaning that I should go in. I had expected to eat in the kitchen. Although I was moved by this sign of respect, this kindness, I was a little nervous going in there among people. I felt they would all know that I was a fugitive. I thought they would recognize me as the ex-Acting Minister of Information, or simply as a Complexer, and when the photographs of me and the notices about my disappearance arrived in that town, they would recognize me and report that I had been seen there working as a waitress in a restaurant. I had decided that that was what I definitely wanted to do. That lottery ticket vendor and that cook had been kinder to me than my own relatives on the Mountain, and I could not face walking on alone again. The vendor was inside the restaurant hovering about the tables selling his COMPLOT tickets, but waiting for me to come.

I sat at a table in a back corner, and he came over.

"Thank you for the shoes and the skirt," I said.

He just nodded, as if he possibly had nothing to do with those gifts. He stood there as they brought me several dishes of food. And I ate it all, trying to use the etiquette of the Fielders, not mixing the different kinds of food and taking equally from each dish in turn, so that no dish or type of food would be affronted at being first or last, favored or disfavored. I became quite engrossed in this exercise, taking each mouthful in an orderly and premeditated way, and I began to understand a little how the Fielders respect the various foods that they grow and how the food itself becomes a powerful force and needs prayers and supplication.

While I was eating like that, carefully watching my food, I heard a noise outside. Three army Jeeps had pulled up. The soldiers in them, about twenty in all, were jumping down into the street and pouring into the restaurant. I went to get up and hide out at the back, but the vendor, who had been watching me all the time, stood in the way.

"Where are you going?" he asked. And he stood near me, forcing me to keep on eating. I was terrified. I knew the Complex must be looking for me. And I had to sit there eating that food while the soldiers threw themselves down at the empty tables and called for food. Some of the customers who had been sitting at tables at the front finished their meals quickly and left, the soldiers jeering at them for being afraid. As soon as a table became free, more soldiers spilled around it. They seemed to take up the whole place. I wanted to run away.

The owner of the restaurant came in from the kitchen, looked at the chaos, and said to me, "You want to work? You can start now. You can take their orders and bring them their food, before they tear the place to pieces." And he hurried back to the kitchen. The vendor smiled and nodded. I thought I had made a big mistake, dropping my disguise and trusting these people. They were going to get me into trouble. I had finished my meal. The other waiters were rushing back and forth with food and drink. I stood up slowly, wondering what I should do. I could not see how to disappear without drawing a great deal of attention to myself. I picked up my own dishes and carried them back to the kitchen.

"I could stay out here and wash the dishes," I offered.

"Later," said the owner. "Right now we have to get food into them. The animals. Get these plates out there."

I had to take a tray of plates and glasses out, walk right up to their tables, and set them out before the soldiers. I expected to be arrested on the spot, but they scarcely looked at me. Even their officer, who sat alone at a small table and could be expected to recognize fugitives, scarcely looked at me. Being a servant, a waitress, and a Fielder was another effective disguise. But I was terrified the whole time. I have always hated soldiers and their violent ways and their brutishness, particularly these new types of Complex soldiers, so unlike the ones who fought in the revolution to establish the new order now gone haywire. I was a soldier of sorts, too, I suppose. Although I'm not so sure. I have no valor.

We all shuttled back and forth with dishes, food, drink, cigarettes, hot cloths for their hands and faces, and the vendor did splendidly selling them tickets and telling them ethnic jokes against the Fielders. He winked at me once or twice. As the soldiers got merrier, he even substituted the Military for the Field in his jokes, which made me anxious, but the soldiers laughed harder, until their officer called them outside again. They all went out, threw themselves down on a grassy spot under some trees, and fell asleep for their afternoon nap.

I was in the kitchen by then, washing dishes, thankful to be out of the public eye. The owner gave me some money for the several hours' work I had done, and then I went out to the back, where my old clothes had long been dry. I folded them up into a little pillow and lay down and fell asleep.

The sound of hammering a little way off awakened me. I got up, straightened my clothes, and went to find the ticket vendor. I thought I would pay him back the money he had given me and discuss with him my idea of staying. Having survived the restaurant ordeal, I felt safe again. The thought of traveling on made me ill. I walked through the kitchen, where the owner was just waking up from his own nap. The hammering came from the front and I went to the door of the restaurant, which by then felt a little like my own home, to see what was happening.

The soldiers were all awake and refreshed and were hammering up signs on the town notice boards and on trees and fences. The signs were covered with several small photographs, all under the heading ENECOM, enemy of the Complex. The vendor was out there and he saw me before I was able to duck back inside. Now, I thought, that vendor is going to turn me in. I was certain that my picture was one of those on the poster. All the vendor had to do was call the soldiers over. I went straight out the back, through the kitchen again. The owner had not yet gone out to see what it was all about. As I went past him he said, "We start again for supper in a while. The vegetables need washing and chopping."

I nodded and went out, only to find that the vendor had gone straight around to the back of the restaurant and was waiting for me. I stopped and looked to see where I could run to, but he blocked the way. If I ran back out to the front, the soldiers would see me. I sighed and then the vendor beckoned me to him and we walked through the trees and out into the fields. The hammering had stopped. Then I heard the Jeeps all start up again. They were going east, I guessed, and would now be ahead of me with their signs all along my route, because it was clear to me now that I would have to resume my flight and head for the Mountain again. I hated the thought of all that wandering alone, pretending to be mad, all that hiding and performing.

The vendor walked beside me. I still couldn't guess what he wanted from me or why he had helped me. I remembered the money I had for him and I held it out. He took it, looked at it, then gave it back.

"You should keep it. I can't withdraw an act of charity."

I knew he was right. Not so much about the charity, but about my needing money.

"Why did you help me?" I asked. "Do you know me?"

He shrugged. "Why should I know you? I still have several obligatory kindnesses to perform, that's all."

He had walked with me, led me really, across several fields and through some trees. Ahead lay more fields and in the distance I saw the clouds gathered around the Mountain, and I saw the vague shape of the Mountain itself.

I had become crazy again, muttering, making people step aside to let me pass. I could walk through towns and villages like that, despite the posters, although I never stopped to look at the posters closely, in case someone recognized me. I never actually saw my picture. I scurried past the posters, never even taking a quick look.

I ate from rubbish heaps and raw stuff from the Field. I forgot why I was walking and what I wanted. I just walked. I had found an old basket which I tied around my waist with a strip of cloth. I would put things in it. At one point I had a collection of interesting twigs and stones. Then I did not know why I had them and I threw them out. Possibly I had been thinking that I might need them to make a fire to keep warm, but that is only speculation in retrospect. I had no idea why I was carrying them.

Each day the Mountain got a little closer. Then there was the long, gradual climb. The days were colder, the nights freezing. I thought I would freeze to death. I have heard that death by freezing is about the pleasantest death possible. If you are asleep, you never wake up. If you are awake, you soon stop feeling the cold—I suppose it is a numbness, no feeling at all— and you feel a euphoria, a great happiness and a drowsiness. And you fall asleep and die.

I thought that that was what would happen to me. The picture of Lak that I had been able to carry in my mind had gone. I knew then that I had imagined him and our special closeness. On the first Mountain trip and afterwards, when I was first separated from him, I had been tormented by loneliness for him. But his presence had been strong and I had been able to sustain myself with it. I talked to him in my mind, constantly, and almost expected to see him there whenever I turned around. I could easily see his face, hear his voice, and recreate whole conversations in precise detail. When I remembered the night of the wedding when Lak came back into the house while the sisters waited for him in the car, to tell me he would miss me, I could feel his hands on my arms and I could feel him kissing me. I could feel my cheek against his chest when he held me against him. I could actually feel his shirt on my cheek. Then his letters came, which helped, too. Holding them, rereading certain phrases, seeing his handwriting reminded me that he existed, that he loved me, and that I had not been imagining anything. But now, after the Peninsula, the Island, and walking across the Field endlessly, and having heard nothing from Lak for so long, I knew nothing anymore. I was doubting everything that had ever happened to me. I was thinking that I had manufactured my love for him. My whole past life seemed vague, uncertain. Even *The Sacred Journey* and its lessons seemed like nothing as I walked, though I could remember my obsession with it. What did I care?

I was going to the Mountain to become a hermit, and perhaps to gather physical and moral strength from the volcano. From my relatives I expected little—maybe a bed for a night or two. The tight family bonds of *The Sacred Journey* had disappeared. The family's allegiance was to the Complex and its ephemeral promises. I would go to the Mountain, if I did not die a pleasant death first.

I walked, slept, ate what I could, and walked. I believed that I would die one night and I did not care. I passed through many villages. No one bothered me, until one day, in a village in the foothills, I stumbled over something in the road and fell down, and I could not get up.

Then I found myself in a hospital again. I opened my eyes and asked someone, the doctor perhaps, if everyone had drowned.

"Nobody drowns here," he replied, and even though his voice was abrupt and cold, the information he gave me made me feel so peaceful that I went back to sleep.

I was in the most primitive hospital I had ever seen. It was one big room with about twenty beds in it, with people just lying still on the beds. Some had sheets and blankets. Some had only sheets or pieces of cloth, some had nothing. The patients who had no coverings wrapped themselves up in their clothes. I had no sheets and no mattress, but I was clean, and my clothes were clean again. Someone had washed me, and them. Then I saw outside the window what looked like a little shanty town, an area with makeshift sheets of corrugated iron and plastic, strung out to make tents and small houses. The people of this settlement were cooking over their fires. Children were playing around, and their dogs were wandering about. I saw two pigs snuffling in the dirt. Then I looked back at my fellow patients and saw the man who had told me that no one drowns. The liar. He was making his round. I hated him. I hated his hair, short and crudely cut and sticking out stupidly over his ears. It looked like a bunch of little nails hanging onto a magnet, at all angles.

He had a young man and woman with him, and they went from bed to bed. He looked, nodded, grunted, said a word or two about each case in quick Complex speech to the other two, but he never touched the poor specimens lying there sick in bed. It was clear he could not bear to touch them. When they were opposite me, I saw that they wore plastic bags over their shoes, as if they were making their way through a sewer and did not want to be contaminated. And plastic bags were relatively hard to come by.

They came over toward my bed and stopped beside the man next to me. This poor man, I noticed just then, was extremely ill. He had no bedding, and was lying there on the bare boards. He had bandages around his middle, through which blood had begun to show. Red, fresh blood. This patient turned his eyes to look up at the doctor. The doctor grunted.

"I operated on this one yesterday. Silly bastards. They always come in when it is too late. This place is a hardship post, there is no disputing that, as you will find out for yourselves." And the doctor with the nails for hair lifted up his right hand and brought it down quickly toward the sick man's abdomen, as if he were going to hit it or press right down on the bandages and blood. I felt my own abdomen contract in anticipation of the blow, and I held my breath as if it were I he was about to hit. The doctor stopped his hand just above the man's abdomen. The effect was the same as if he had struck the blow. The sick man's eyes had widened. He, too, had believed that this doctor intended to hit him. He had opened his mouth to let out a little cry and had taken in a breath in fright, and that sudden breath, that sudden contraction of the muscles, caused the wound to bleed again. As I watched, with the doctor's hand still poised above the wound, the fresh bloodstain spread on the bandages.

"Hopeless," said the doctor, and seeing that I was now awake, he came to my bed, the others just behind him. "We found this one out on the road," he said. "Mad." Then to me he said, "You'll have to give us your name, village, and number, you know, if you want to stay here."

I lied to him. I told him I was my cousin Dum, and that I was from Rekkned, and I gave a false number. I spoke in Rekknedese, knowing that he would not be able to hear that I had an accent or spoke haltingly.

"Speak in Complex," he said. "If you are stupid enough to wander so far from your home, you should bring with you the language you'll need in this world."

He turned to the other two quickly. "You'll hate it here, but what can you do? They're all stupid. At least you'll have the new hospital, if it ever gets finished. If they ever stop striking and causing trouble." To me he said loudly, more slowly, "Your family will have to send someone with food and bedding, or you'll starve to death and die of pneumonia, and it won't be our fault." He nodded out the window, indicating, I suppose, that whoever came to take care of me could set up house in that shanty town outside. "Filthy animals," he said to his companions. "When they started working on the hospital they were in rags. Now, with the wages they're getting and the gifts and clothes from the Complex contractors, they are prospering, and the more they prosper, the more they cause trouble. I sometimes think we should all just pack up and go back and forget all about them. The hell with development."

Then he caught sight of the two pigs. I thought he was going to have a stroke on the spot. He took two strides to the window, leaned out and started screaming, "I thought I warned you that the next time I found pigs near my hospital I'd shoot them."

He walked, ran, out of the ward into a little room at the end. He came out with a rifle. Several of the shanty town people had grabbed hold of the pigs and were pulling them away. The pigs were squealing and resisting. They knocked down one of the little huts. A pot of soup that had been cooking over one of the little open fires spilled and extinguished the fire. The doctor rushed back to my window with his rifle. He bent over, rested an elbow on the window sill, took aim, and fired. He fired two shots, one for each pig. Then he went and stood at the end of the ward and cleaned out his rifle. The man in the bed next to me was crying and bleeding more.

The people outside gathered around the dead pigs. They were talking, shouting, looking up at the windows. The young man and woman, the new doctors, stood by looking somewhat surprised. I heard the woman say to the man, "Did you know that one pig here costs the same as a bride? We got that in our orientation hour."

The people outside blocked the dead pigs from my view. Then I saw them moving off, one by one, with chunks of meat in their hands. The pigs' owners were hacking up the dead animals and selling the meat.

The doctor came back to us, looking pleased with himself. "That's the only way to get something into their heads."

He will be killed some day. An accident of some sort, like a rock on his head or a scalpel through the heart. I would like to have killed him myself.

That night I walked out. Nobody cared. I had no one to take care of me and I was not really sick, just exhausted. In spite of the constant nightmare of the journey, I felt optimistic once more. I think that this was because I had slept and was clean, and the cruelty and insanity of the doctor had reminded me that the resisters still had a lot to do. I just walked out, with my things rolled up.

It was dusk. On a back road that seemed to lead toward the

Mountain, I came across a crowd of villagers who had gathered for some kind of meeting. I stood and listened. It appeared that they were the laborers for the new hospital and were striking. When I asked someone why they were striking, he said, ''Prices are going up and up.'' I learned that none of the eighty laborers had gone to work that day. They all said they were sick or had family business to see to. Fifteen had been fired, to frighten the others back to work. The doctor, who I gathered was acting as go-between between the Complex contractors and the local labor, since he was supposed to know the ways of the locals, had announced that if the workers did not return, the contractors would go back to the Complex and there would be no more hospital and no more work and no more wages. I knew that he was bluffing, but the villagers believed him. The villagers were not organized. They appeared to have no leader or spokesman, and no clear idea of what to do next. They were milling about on the road and grumbling about rising prices and the mad doctor. They had struck because they wanted more money, but now they were saying that it was because the doctor had shot the pigs, which meant economic ruin for the owners of the pigs. They seemed to take this to be a sign that they should go back to work, logic that was hard for me to follow.

I found myself suddenly calling for attention. I thought I sounded a bit like the doctor himself. ''Listen, you are all stupid to be talking like this,'' I said. ''The Complex contractors need you. Without you, they can't build the hospital, and they have to build the hospital or they won't get their money, and you can be sure that they are expecting to be given a fortune to buy their bricks, cement, and timber, and you can be sure that they put a great deal of that fortune in their own pockets. They need you so that a hospital can be built and they can get rich. If no workers come, no bricklaying, no cement mixing, nothing can be done. Use the strength that you have. Use the strike to get more money, and use it to topple the doctor.''

Topple. It was odd to hear my voice using a word like that. A

Complex propaganda word. I spent some time talking with them, suggesting how they might organize and present demands. Then I left and went on my way. I hope they succeeded, and I hope that doctor has had his accident.

In all that walking I did not steal a van or a car or even a bicycle, partly because I did not want to steal from good people like the Fielders, partly because I did not really believe that my personal mission—because that is what it was, a running away for my own personal survival, not for any political or greater cause—warranted such a theft, but mainly I did not steal because I was likely to be pursued as a thief and caught if I did. Once, when I was visiting a friend, long ago now, in the Complex, a passer-by leaned in the window of a room at the front of the house and picked up a purse which my friend had left on the desk. She and I walked into the room and saw the purse disappearing. We leaned out the window and yelled, "Thief! Thief!" then ran out into the street ourselves. A crowd of people pursued the thief and retrieved the purse. Then they attacked him and actually tore him to pieces. The thief was from a different area. I had forgotten all about that until I contemplated theft myself. And then the memory of yelling out, "Thief! Thief!" and running up to the crowd and seeing the terrible sight of a body dismembered in such a short time became clear again. I am a coward, and did not want to get hurt.

I walked up the Mountain and instead of following the roads with their hairpin turns I scrambled straight up, crossing the road and going into the trees and undergrowth, then crossing the road again. There was even the trace of a little path, straight up. It could have been the very path that the ancient fugitives used.

The path was much faster than the road, but I had begun to get scratched and bruised, since I was crawling up on my hands and knees a lot of the time. I had to rest often. Higher up there were still patches of ice on the road and I slipped once, losing my balance and falling down hard on my knee and then over onto my hip and hand. I picked myself up immediately. Then the shock of the fall and the hurt made me lean against a tree at the edge of the road, and I cried. I cried because my knee and my hand were scraped and bleeding and my hip ached. I seem to have been crying ever since that first trip to the Mountain. Before that, never.

It is funny about delayed shock. In books and films when people are hurt, they rarely cry. They seem to grit their teeth, and give a small groan, a grimace, and then they carry on. Yet when I fall I find that my body is out of my control and needs to cry to heal itself, to recover from the shock, and to get fit to continue. Once I saw a woman walking along in the Complex, about to cross the street. She tripped on something and fell down. She was well dressed and clearly held some kind of reputable job. But down she went like any ordinary person, in her good clothes, and rolled over on her back. I hurried over to help her but she had picked herself up quickly and was dusting herself down and laughing, as if to say, "Aren't I silly to trip like that?" But I could see that she had had a heavy fall. By the time I got to her side she was making a big show of looking at her shoe, turning her foot this way and that, blaming it for her clumsiness.

"Are you all right?" I asked. "You should sit down for a minute."

But she hated my concern and attention. She gave me a look, still laughing, and said, "It was nothing. These stupid shoes." And she crossed the street. But on the other side I saw that she had to steady herself against a fence.

My fall on the ice seemed to demolish me again. I held onto the tree and cried. "What am I doing here?" I said aloud. "What do I think I'm trying to do? From where to where? No one knows where I am, no one cares. I'm going to get to Rekkned and they're going to wonder what I'm doing there. They don't want me there."

I thought of lying down and trying to die. But of course, after a while, I started off again up the Mountain. It was cold, but I had stopped feeling it.

Then the rain started to pour down and sweep over the road and mountainside. It was useless to try and keep dry, since there was no shelter. The rain seemed to be able to penetrate any tree covering. Then I heard a car below me, slowly making its way up the hill. I decided to risk hitching a ride. I scrambled onto the road and stood on the little straight stretch between the hairpin turns and I waited ten or fifteen minutes in the rain, until the car rounded the bend.

It was a Jeep, and it was full of soldiers. And behind it was another Jeep and an army truck, all packed with soldiers. I just stood there. I could not believe my stupidity.

"Get that one," someone in the first Jeep called. The driver slowed down and two soldiers jumped down. They easily caught me and brought me to the Jeep, which had not actually stopped. I suppose that, because of the steepness of the grade, it was possible that if they stopped they would never get started again. The soldiers still in the Jeep leaned down and pulled me up and the two who had caught me hoisted themselves back on.

"You're just what we need," they said. "Take us to where the resisters are hiding out."

"I don't know what you're talking about," I said. And I did not. "I am on my way home to my family in Rekkned." I told my story, giving my cousin's name and a false number. I spoke first in Rekknedese, to prove I was a local, then in the Complex language so that they would understand.

It was getting darker. With the rain pouring down and sweeping over the road we almost sailed up the road, which was just wide enough for a single lane of traffic. The truck behind us took up the whole road. We had no roof and no doors. We bounced along at all angles to the road, and I had to concentrate on holding on. I imagine a ride on a wild horse would be much the same. I hoped if I was tossed out it would be into a patch of soft grass and not when we were crossing a ravine. One of the soldiers actually was thrown out of the Jeep. He fell down the slope at the side of the road for a little way, then picked himself up and ran limping after us. We slowed down again so that he could climb back on. This little incident made them tie me to a bar at the back of the driver's seat, so that they would not lose me. They said it was out of concern for a civilian's safety. But they clearly did not care for my story. "We'll take you right home, then," they said when I told them where I was from. "You shouldn't be out alone like this. It's dangerous at this time of day. Resisters everywhere." And so we roared slowly along the road through the dripping, glistening trees, the air solid with rain.

They took me all the way to Rekkned, right to the house of Pab and Upi, who of course were astounded to see me. They were in the middle of piling food and clothes into baskets, and I realized that the holy day of the Rekknedese must be approaching, the day they go up and throw things into the crater. I had heard, during my last visit there, that they now hired young men to take the stuff up and throw it in, giving them ten percent of what was in the baskets, rather than going all that way themselves.

"What are you doing here?" they called.

"I'm back, Father and Mother," I answered, trying to imply that I was a daughter who had been on a journey.

"What's she doing here?" they asked the soldiers.

The soldiers asked if I was the cousin I said I was.

"Of course not," they answered and produced the very cousin Dum, who recited her own number and showed her identity card. "But we've been hearing about this one," they said, nodding at me. "We certainly did not expect her here, bringing us bad fortune."

And that was it. The soldiers made me their prisoner. I thought of getting to the volcano and jumping in, but I couldn't escape. They took me to the police station in Rekkned, a grubby little shack that served as office and living quarters for the three-man Rekkned police force. A clothesline with a blanket pegged to it was strung across the middle of the shack, dividing the two areas. A pimply little policeman was sitting there reading a comic book.

"An arrest," said the soldiers.

"We're closed until tomorrow," the policeman said. "We'll do it in the morning."

The policeman seemed delighted at the prospect of an arrest, a bit of action. But he must have wanted to get full value from the experience and string it out a little. He did not take his feet down from the desk or stop reading his comic adventure.

"You can have the rest house tonight, and we'll make the arrest official tomorrow," the policeman said.

The soldiers seemed to understand this whole procedure. So there I was in the rest house again overnight, freezing, and tied to my bed.

The following morning we returned to the police station. The men were not dressed when we walked in. The policeman of the previous night and two others were in their underpants on the other side of the hanging blanket fiddling with the fire. There was a scuffle when we came in, and eventually they emerged, more or less dressed, and took out their pieces of paper and stamps and ink, and everything they might possibly need. One of them sharpened pencils with a knife from the living quarters. It took them five minutes to write a dozen words, that is, the time, date, place, then another five to get my name, which the family had happily supplied at the request of the soldiers. Then they had to search for the right forms, the filling out of which took possibly an hour.

Outside I could see the horses loaded with food and clothing for the crater, and I watched the assortment of young men gather and lead them off. This was the day I had always longed for, when I could at last be part of a tradition. And Lak, in that first puzzling letter of his, had urged me, instructed me almost, not to miss a festival. I had always believed it was this Mountain ritual, this holy day, that he wanted me to return to. And there I was, in Rekkned for the holy day, as if by design, and in Rekkned on the holy day I was arrested.

We started off down the Mountain back to the Complex. I was an official prisoner, now tied even more securely by a rope tied around my waist and fastened to the seat in the back of the Jeep. The rain had stopped, although everything was still wet. The drivers were extremely happy to have accomplished something, the capture of me. They went far too fast for the road, competing I think to see who could be the most daring. They sounded their horns, as if we were returning from a jolly, all-night party.

I was swung from side to side and eventually vomited over the side of the Jeep, feeling sicker than I have ever felt in my life. The soldiers hooted and jeered at me and held their noses. My Jeep was first, with the other Jeep and the truck pressing behind, forcing us to go faster and faster.

"They're making me go too fast," our driver said, but there was no room for him to pull to one side to let them pass, and he went faster.

We rounded one of the bends with our tires squealing, to find ourselves on a patch of ice and in front of us a little wooden trestle with a notice on it, "DONT," in Rekknedese, and an arrow pointing us around it. There must have been a pothole or something. To avoid hitting the trestle the driver turned the steering wheel and braked, all too suddenly. It would have been impossible not to have had an accident. Either we could have run straight into the trestle and crashed, or we could have tried to avoid it and crashed. At the speed we were going, we simply skidded and sailed off the side of the road through the air. It seemed we traveled a beautiful slow, long arc. I remember looking back and seeing the other Jeep and the truck, as if drawn in our wake, also sailing into the air after us. Soldiers were flung in all directions, also sailing through the air, but not me, tied to the seat. I just sat there. I remember puzzling about the word

"DONT" and deducing that it must have been written by someone who did not know Rekknedese well, because there was no such word as "dont." It should have been "dovit," meaning deviation, and whoever had written it down had got the "V" and the "I" joined into a back-to-front "N."

I remember feeling exhilarated. I remember finally crashing, then turning and tumbling, down and down, and I remember feeling thankful that at last I was going to die.

The Jeep came to rest and I was still sitting in the back seat. No one else was in the Jeep with me. It was very warm. I thought that perhaps the whole thing was on fire and I was going to burn to death—very appropriate, since I had already escaped death by drowning and freezing. But it was the sun streaming down which caused the heat and made me close my eyes again as soon as I opened them. The Jeep was resting against a clump of trees, and as I opened my eyes again, slowly, I saw that they were bamboos, green bamboos, that had bent with the Jeep's impact and stopped its fall. Out the other side of the Jeep I saw grass and flowers, and even little birds hopping here and there, and on the hood and the steering wheel.

I was hurting a great deal, and when I went to move, I felt the rope around my waist pull tight. Little bits of glass were everywhere, on my lap, on the seat, in my hair. I was lucky not to have been torn in half. So I just waited, expecting I don't know what. I just waited, with my eyes closed, listening to the sounds around me, and not moving at all. I was slowly arriving at the conclusion that I had fallen into the narrow valley with the microclimate that cut back into the Mountain, the little summer ravine we had crossed on the way up to Rekkned the first time. Then I heard footsteps on the grass, and someone climbing into the Jeep. And I felt my ropes being cut. I was lifted and carried away from the Jeep and lowered onto the grass under a tree. When I felt the grass beneath me I opened my eyes, and I saw Lak's face, bending over me. That lovely face.

I reached up to touch him and he smiled and kissed my fingers. He bent down to me and kissed my cheek lightly, and he whispered in my ear, "My Neila."

I could not talk. The tears slid out of my eyes down my cheeks, and I was crying for what seemed like the hundredth time for the hundredth different reason. I lay there, holding his hand, and he lay beside me. We said nothing, but just stayed like that. Every now and then I opened my eyes and found Lak still there, just looking at me, his serious face warm and loving. Then he started to talk, whispering, although there was no one else around.

"My brilliant Neila," he whispered, "to end up here, exactly according to plan. I couldn't stop them setting up that trestle ambush, and I didn't know you were with that convoy. How could I have known that you would arrive like that?"

I smiled, loving his voice, not knowing what he was talking about. He carried me away from the wreck, down a slope to a flat area at the top of one of the river banks, shaded by bamboos and other tropical growth, and he laid me on a bamboo mat under a cloth awning. I could hear the river rushing past below. Lak disappeared over the edge of the bank, sliding down to get me some water in a little container. Later, after I could sit up and move around a little, I saw that the bank was almost perpendicular, and I used to like watching Lak climb down using a couple of roots that stuck out of the bank as hand-holds. At the water's edge he would squat with both feet on one root, one hand holding onto another root that formed a loop, and lea... out over the deep, swiftly flowing river and fill our little bucket. It was a climb of three meters at least and he could climb down, lean out, and bring the water back in a minute or so. He was as agile as a wild animal.

"How did you send those letters?" I remember croaking, as if it were the paramount thing I had to ascertain. It was the first thing that I could remember to ask about. "How were you able to do that?"

"I was a prisoner in the back room of a post office on the

Peninsula," Lak said. We both started to laugh. "I was even there when you were there. I read about your progress, but I was a prisoner."

I thought I would die laughing this time. But it hurt my bruises and cuts too much and I used my foolproof method, biting my lip, to stop. "Don't tell me any stories that are funny," I begged. "But what about the Mountain language? How could you possibly know it?"

"Because of the official policy on the ethnics, there is a set of regional tour guides in all post offices," Lak said, and we started laughing again, gasping for breath. We were lying side by side, Lak resting on one elbow looking down at me and I with my head against his shirt, biting my lip and trying not to laugh.

I remained weak and dizzy for many days and I could stay awake for only an hour or so at a time. I found it hard to talk and think clearly, and I could remember very little before the accident. I just wanted to sleep for years. It was only much later that I could piece together the terrible trauma of the Jeep accident, all those months of walking, the escape from the Complex, the Island, the Peninsula drownings, all that harassment from Serena after the disappearance of the family and Lak, and all those farcical group meetings which I had taken so literally and seriously, sneaking out from the family, whom I always believed to be loyal Complexers.

And then one night the volcano erupted. Lak had stayed by me constantly, making me rest in the shade on the mat. He slid down the bank every morning to catch fish and bring back a pitcher of water to boil for tea, squatting on those roots and leaning far out. He combed my hair, and then let me fall asleep again. He lay beside me and talked to me, helping me recall our earlier times at home, saying, "Remember how you used to come with me to listen to the radio?" and "Remember how you used to wait for me at the front of the house and I used to hope that you were there?" And I began to remember the earlier times but not much of the immediate past.

I was totally happy there in the microclimate with Lak.

There were other resisters in the little valley, camped a little farther downstream, even some from the Island who had been on that ferry. They were all resting and preparing themselves for new action. A kind of furlough had been declared, and our little valley had the air of a holiday resort, a nature club. Gradually I was able to take part in the evening talks, when everyone gathered along the river bank and dropped stones into the water and talked about what they were going to do. They talked about the past and about beginning the resistance again, which I dreaded, and Lak jotted down things in the little notebook he carried in his shirt pocket.

They had used the bamboo which grew so abundantly to make everything they needed: poles for their tents, woven mats, spears to catch fish, and skewers to roast the little fish pieces over tiny fires. They had also placed sharpened bamboo sticks in the undergrowth all around our camp, so that any stranger approaching would be impaled. My Jeep must have sailed right over them.

The banks of the river were so steep and slippery that I was unable to get down to fetch water myself and catch fish. But as I grew stronger and less dizzy I was able to sharpen the bamboo skewers for roasting the fish. I sharpened several hundred and piled them up near our tent, since I wanted to feel I was contributing something.

Then, as I began seeing more clearly, I suddenly remembered the sisters and Mother on the Island. Lak and I were lying on our mat and for the first time I had not fallen asleep as soon as I had lain down. I turned to Lak and slid my hands inside his shirt.

"I just remembered," I said. "I found your sisters and Mother. They're on the Island."

"I know that," he said.

"But I actually saw them," I said. "I talked to them. They were in a terrible way. Mother especially. But we cleared up the past misunderstandings about one another, although they still distrust me. And they told me about your escape." My head was against Lak's chest and I could feel his notebook in the pocket of his shirt against my cheek. My hands were pressed against his back, holding him tightly to me. I was remembering Mother and that nightmare Island. "How lucky that you at least escaped and you weren't carried off that night with them, even though you got caught later."

"Don't be silly," he said. "It wasn't luck."

I drew back a little from him. "What do you mean?"

He just looked down at me, half smiling. That was when the volcano erupted, angry, I trust, because of the insincere offering of the Rekknedese on their holy day and also because of what I was going to learn from Lak. We heard the noise, dull sounds in the distance as if we were being attacked by bombers. Then, as we all gathered in the clearing, ash started to fall into our valley. Luckily, when there is ash there is little lava. I thought at the time that there could easily be some kind of connection underground or aboveground between our valley, which was more like a fissure, and the inside of the Mountain and that lava could have reached us. I spent that night unable to sleep, watching the ash fall down in a ghostly way in the dark. When Lak awoke I finally whispered, "You mean you knew your family would be taken away that night?"

"Of course I did, just as you did," he said. "Remember, you had left on your little vacation that very day, too."

Outside our awning everything was white. Lak got up and climbed down to the river to wash and collect the day's water. Lak's shirt was beside me on the mat and I went through its pockets. I found a tightly folded piece of paper, which I spread out. Lak had written this note:

Vostro, my sweet one, how is your situation there? Good, I hope. All of us in this house are safe and well. Make good use of this present I am sending.

176

And with the note there were a hand-drawn map of the valley with our camp marked on it and a list of the names of all the resisters who had taken refuge in the valley.

Vostro. Serena.

When Lak climbed back up, I was still sitting on the mat under the awning, the papers in my hand, just sitting. I looked up at him. The ash was floating past his face and lodging in his hair and eyebrows.

"How will you send these?" I finally asked, holding up the papers.

"You will take them, or I will," he said. "Since this time I do not have access to our Complex's postal facilities." When I did not laugh at this joke of ours, he sat down beside me and put his arms around me. "Neila, what's wrong? I want you to take them back to the Complex, when all this stuff stops coming down. You will be strong enough. You're certainly clever enough to get them back."

I was having trouble piecing it all together. "How long were you a prisoner in that post office?" was all I could bring myself to ask.

"Three months," he said. "Long enough to learn that language of yours."

"Whose prisoner were you?" That was the question I had been trying to form since the night before.

"Theirs. I was Anny and Leo's hostage. Leo had escaped from Serena. They were as bored as I was with it all. They were waiting for the resistance to succeed and I was waiting to be rescued. They learned the Mountain language, too. The three of us had nothing to do. They made me write to you in it. They knew you would be the only one in the Complex who could read it, and they didn't really think I could use it effectively. I kept hoping that my mentioning their names in those letters would alert you to my plight and that somehow you could trace me and get help to me."

"I tried," I said. "Everything I did was for you."

"Or at least that you could get Serena to help. But it turned out all right," he went on. "The Complex came to the area and recaptured it, Leo and Anny, too. I got away on my own and came here, looking for the resister groups I knew were somewhere around here. When I found these people, they took me in. I was in bad shape and I said I had come from the Island, and since I saw what an opportunity this was, I thought I would gather what information I could. And then you turned up."

Lak had put his shirt on and he bent down to comb my hair for me. I remembered the courtship ritual of my Mountain people with their combs, although I no longer had any family to help me with the ceremony. I still have not heard what had happened to the settlements on the Mountain after the eruption, and whether my relatives there are homeless or dead. Several dead bodies have turned up in the river, carried down from farther up the Mountain. But we have not been able to tell how they died.

"I wish I could have let you know that I was on your side," Lak was saying. "I knew you were there to report on my family. Remember how Father kept track of us all the time? But Serena knew all this, and she warned me about that night, before you all left."

"Your Vostro," I said, bitter.

Lak smiled. Then after a while I said, "Now, these people in this valley, who we have lived with for so many weeks, who took us both in, you want me to help you get them rounded up?"

"Yes," said Lak. "And you can do it. You have been brilliant, pretending to be a resister." He pulled my hair back from my forehead and turned my face to him and kissed me. "By letting you escape like that, by putting your face on that poster that is all over the country, they knew you would lead them to more resisters. But that accident almost wiped you out, and in the line of duty, too. A bit careless of you." He kissed me again. "We might have lost you altogether."

Lak gave me the comb and sat next to me so that I could

comb the ash out of his hair. "I think the resistance will soon be crushed, once and for all," he said.

I was dizzy again, of course. This was the man I had loved for so long, so strongly. This was the man who had allowed the family who adored him to be carried off, all in the line of duty.

The ash came down for several days, covering the grass, the leaves, our clothes, everything, so that the whole landscape turned white. Even the rushing water was filled with it and we had to strain our drinking water and boil it because of those bodies. The path down to the river had become treacherous, the mud mixing with the ash and forming a particularly slippery chute. Lak's hair and eyebrows as he lay beside me were always white, and sometimes if I only half-opened my eyes, he looked like Barm himself. I wanted the whiteness to be a good sign. It was very beautiful and I wanted it to tell me that all would be well, that I would have the courage to do what I had to do, and that life would renew itself. I knew Lak was impatient for me to recover. He wanted me to set out for the Complex and give the names and the map to Serena.

I collected and sharpened more little sticks, slightly larger than the cooking skewers. I made them as sharp as needles. I had them all piled up at my side of the mat, and I hid a knife I took from one of the other resisters under the mat. I also collected pebbles and rocks. I told Lak that the pebbles and sticks were weapons. We could never know when we might need them. Actually I was not certain just what I might have to do with them.

I braided a length of rope with some long bamboo strips. In the middle of the night, I tied the rope to a root at the top of the bank and with great difficulty climbed down to the water's edge, holding tightly to it. I squatted, holding the rope. Then, using the kinfe, I hacked through both ends of the root that formed the loop that Lak used as a hand-hold when he fetched water. I poked the loop back into the bank, so that it looked as if it had not been tampered with. I climbed back to our mat, untied the rope, and lay there until morning, waiting for Lak to get up and go through his morning ritual. My intention was for him to grab onto the loop as usual, for the loop to come loose, for him to fall into the river, get swept away, and drown.

Lak woke up and kissed me. He even said he was sorry our happy time together was coming to an end. Then he took the bucket and disappeared over the edge of the bank. I lay there and heard nothing. I was ready to use the skewers and stones and knife if he should come crawling back up the bank. He would know that I had cut the root and I would have to act fast. But nothing happened. I crawled to the edge and looked over. The root had come out of the bank. There was no sign of Lak.

I lie on the mat expecting to hear from the other resisters that they have found Lak's body in the river downstream. I lie here waiting, and planning what I have to do. I know I have to make sure that the dead for whom I am responsible are disposed of properly, according to the instructions in the sacred book. I shall do what I have to do, and then start the struggle all over again.